Cane & Able
Save He Who Has the Mark

Dean M. Lichterman

CANE AND ABLE

Save He Who Has the Mark

Dean M. Lichterman

Christian Publishing House
Professional Christian Publishing of the Good News!

ISBN-13: **978-0692493618**

ISBN-10: **0692493611**

Christian Publishing House

Cambridge, Ohio

CANE AND ABLE: *Save He Who Has the Mark*

Acknowledgments

Thank you God for providing me with the ability to write.

Thank you to Dave Shea, a true patron of the arts

Also to Rob Carey for the cover photo of Canandaigua Lake

And thank you to the anonymous proofreader

Table of Contents

Chapter 1

Don Lamplighter sat face to face with his new archenemy.

"King's pawn to king four," yelled Ken Knight as he walked onto the concrete playing surface.

Today they were opponents in a heated game of chess on a hot late-June day at a park in Clifton Springs, New York. Just over a week ago they faced off in a much bigger game.

"King's pawn to king four," replied Lamplighter as he then approached the board to move the knee-high pieces.

He sat back down on what is known as the black bench to match the color he was assigned for this contest. The two had a brief, but intense, stare-down.

Knight, who is known to the world as a billionaire financial wizard, took his turn.

"King's knight to king's bishop three," he said before making his move.

To Lamplighter, however, his opponent is also known as Absalom, the local leader of a global Satanic cult bent on taking over the world in the name of what they claim as their beloved father.

"Spanish style," replied Lamplighter as he headed to the pieces to make his counter move. "Something I have seen thousands of times before."

Knight sat back with a grin.

"A system I have used thousands of times before," he replied on the way to move his bishop.

The dapperly dressed Lamplighter made his move and sat right back down just as Knight's laptop computer made a loud beep.

"Something more important than this game, I gather," said Lamplighter. "Perhaps another global crisis awaits your attention."

Knight glared at Lamplighter without saying a word. He then tilted his head to the side as if to ask a question, shook his head and lifted up his laptop.

"I always have to know what my investments are doing," said Knight as he buried his head into the screen. "But I assure you I have the intellect to handle both the markets and your game at the same time."

"You must think that you are pretty smart," said Lamplighter, who leaned forward and rested his head on his cane.

Knight stood up.

"I have never heard of you playing from any of my typical chess opponents," he said as he walked forward to the board. "I can, therefore, conclude that you are not in my league in this game."

Knight then castled. Lamplighter fought against that by advancing his pawn toward his enemy's now-fortified position.

"What are you doing?" asked a visibly frustrated Knight. "I have never seen a board set up like that."

"That's the point. I call it Wing Chung chess," replied Lamplighter. "The same as my fighting style. The strategy of no strategy."

Lamplighter was a 43-year-old struggling freelance journalist. He was in town to conduct an interview with a cancer doctor at the local hospital. Lamplighter had some time between the end of the discussion and the arrival of his bus back to his home in Canandaigua, so he took the opportunity to come to the park for a quick game.

He never expected to see Knight on the other side of the board.

"That's OK," said Knight. "I need a good challenge."

Knight is only 26 years old. He started out as a computer hacker. He became adept at stealing smaller amounts of money and laundering it through investment schemes. Knight made an even bigger profit by offering those services to local crime bosses. Once he all of them as clients, they elected him as their leader at the age of just 23.

Two years ago, Knight met fellow billionaires at an exclusive Caribbean resort. It was then that he and his captains were invited into the world-wide enterprise.

"Lucky you ran into me," replied Lamplighter as he made yet another chess play that not even he expected to make just one move before.

They were playing a blitz style timed game with each side having a total of five minutes to make all of his moves. One wins the contest with a checkmate, resignation or by outlasting the opponent. Lamplighter was a shade under six feet and a slightly out-of-shape 250 pounds. He also walked with a cane, which gave him a disadvantage against his younger and more mobile foe.

The two had exchanged several moves before Lamplighter made a glaring error that cost him a rook.

"I expected that I would eventually get into the lead somehow," laughed Knight. "But I admit that you have lasted longer than almost everyone else I have played here."

"What exactly are you going here?" inquired Lamplighter.

"I know some doctors and retired professors who live in this village," Knight replied before glancing at his laptop and making a quick check of his gold options. "I am here every Monday morning to see who shows up."

On cue, one of his regular opponents, a former math professor, grabbed a spot on the hill to watch the show.

"First time I've been here," said Lamplighter. "I'm just here after an assignment."

Knight seethed at that last comment.

"That explains the shirt and tie," he responded.

Knight was angry because Lamplighter said the exact same thing after rescuing a baby from a car stuck on train tracks two Mondays ago. The baby's mother was already dead. The intervention for the baby kept Knight from helping a phony pastor friend of his cover up a long-past adulterous encounter that suddenly reappeared.

Lamplighter's investigation led to a solution of the case, but Knight and his murderous colleagues were able to hide all of the evidence. The pastor committed suicide, leaving no tie to Knight.

The two conversed after the event, leaving Knight convinced that Lamplighter did not know about his connections to that particular crime. What Knight did not know was that Lamplighter hid and caught a glimpse of Knight's Absalom identity, and has made it his mission to prove it.

"I see you are scrambling for cover," sniveled Knight as his incessant attacks kept making Lamplighter's position harder and harder to defend.

Each player made four more moves. Lamplighter made yet another escape when the alarm on his bench blared, giving the victory to Knight.

"Looks like you have run out of time," Knight grinned.

Just then, the bus made its scheduled stop at the park, the driver waiting for passengers right next to Knight's black limousine.

"Nope," replied Lamplighter as he headed for his ride home. "I am right on schedule."

Chapter 2

"I'm scared, Mr. Lamplighter," whispered the elderly lady that eased herself into the bus seat next to him.

"What's going on?" replied Lamplighter, matching the volume level of his new-found seat companion.

"You help people, right?" she asked. "That is what the news said that you do."

Lamplighter looked down and shook his head.

"If I can," he replied while looking at his cane and wondering into what mess he was about to get himself. "What seems to be the trouble?"

"See those three gentlemen back there?" she asked. "Those three guys, all about your size?"

Wanting to conceal the conversation, Lamplighter kept his head down as the bus headed north out of the village.

"I saw them when I got on the bus," he noted. "Why?"

"They got on the bus in Geneva and were saying some awfully dirty things," she said as she started blushing. "Things a proper lady like me wouldn't repeat."

The bus was driven by John. Lamplighter had yet to meet this driver, only knowing his name from the driver's name tag. John left the lot at the park and made a right-hand turn to head out of the village. He followed that with a left-hand turn into the parking lot of a strip mall. The three men glared at Lamplighter as they exited.

"Hold the bus," said the tallest of the three. "We're thirsty. Just going to the store for something to drink."

"She's right," thought Lamplighter as he observed one of the men make a call on his cell phone. 'They are about my size."

"Here's the thing," she continued. "I think they were talking about doing things with those young girls that got on the bus before."

She looked past Lamplighter out the window to see if any of the men were returning.

"With the news talking about those missing girls over the past couple of weeks," she said in a more audible range. "Well, like I said, I'm scared."

"I don't blame you," replied Lamplighter. "Let's see what they are going to do here."

Lamplighter remembered the girls. They got on the bus with Lamplighter and the elderly woman at the start of the route in Canandaigua at 8 a.m. All five of them remained on the first part of the trip from the central transfer station, north to Shortsville and Manchester. The route then featured an eastward turn onto Highway 96 for a stop at a trailer park before visiting the backside of a travel oasis on Interstate 90.

The girls got off the bus at the oasis.

The next stop after the oasis was same store where they are now. This was followed by a jaunt through downtown Clifton Springs, where Lamplighter left the bus the first time through. It then traveled out of the village, through Phelps and turned south to several stops in Geneva before turning around for the return trip.

This meant that next stop would be the oasis.

"I would like to help you," replied Lamplighter. "But in order to know what to do next, I have to know what they said."

"I don't want to repeat that," replied the lady.

"That I understand. I try to act Godly and gentlemanly myself," he replied. "But if you want to help these girls, and perhaps God knows who else. The best thing to do is tell me what they said."

The woman blushed again.

"It was about sex," whispered the lady.

Lamplighter barely heard her as she turned her head down.

'They wanted to have sex with those young girls," she continued. "Can you do something?"

Lamplighter nodded in agreement before taking out his cell phone and making a call. He hung up just as the three men rejoined the trip

"Thanks man," this time the shortest of the trio spoke. "We have business at the Oasis and don't have time for shopping in their gift shop."

Each member of the group had a soda in each hand.

Lamplighter and the lady looked at each other and just nodded. If they were right, the next couple minutes of the trip were going to be very dangerous.

The girls were waiting on a picnic table outside of the Oasis as the bus pulled into the lot. A chain-link fence divided off the area to prevent cars from leaving the interstate without paying a toll. Workers at the restaurants inside the rest area were able to pass through a gate in the fence in order to use the parking lot on the Highway 96 side.

"Yes," exclaimed one of the men as they stood up to leave the bus.

He was quickly silenced by the other two as the made their exit and made a beeline in the direction of the girls. Watching this proved to Lamplighter that he needed to act. He didn't like the odds of a three-on-one fight, but seeing no other option, he followed the men out. The lady next to him held her hand up, into which Lamplighter placed his cell phone on the way by.

The men had a lead on Lamplighter, who took advantage of the gap to form a quick plan. He decided to get their attention by pretending that they left something on the bus, but didn't have time to shout as the youngest of the girls made a sprint for the protection of the vehicle. It was the break he needed as the smallest of the men gave chase. Lamplighter stood in the path of the attacker to allow the girl to get on the bus as the driver shut the door.

"You are going to pay for that, fatso," yelled the man as he threw a clumsy right-handed haymaker that Lamplighter easily dodged.

Without saying a word, Lamplighter retaliated with a sharp left-handed chop to the throat. It immediately sent the attacker to the ground.

"One down, one saved," he thought. "Two more of each to go."

The middle-sized of the three men made his move toward Lamplighter as the biggest of the three bear hugged one of the girls to prevent an escape. Lamplighter was curious as to why the oldest girl didn't try to escape, but the thought was interrupted by the second kidnapper.

"You are going to pay for that, idiot," he said as he drew a pocket knife.

Lamplighter began spinning his cane as the two circled each other. A crowd from the oasis gathered with several cell phones aimed toward the action.

The man suddenly charged Lamplighter, who evaded the attack by stepping to his right, nearly causing the kidnapper to fall on his face.

"Pffff," scoffed Lamplighter.

This made his attacker even angrier. He barreled toward Lamplighter even faster. The second attempt was thwarted by Lamplighter sidestepping to the left and delivering a cane strike to the back of the neck. The blow didn't send the kidnapper to the ground, but Lamplighter took care of that by diving for a takedown at the attacker's knees and quickly applying a full nelson.

"I've never seen a sorrier collection of wuss bags in my life," said Lamplighter while staring at the third man, awaiting the next move. "Is this why you have to take young girls?"

The hold allowed the unguarded girl to make a dead run and reach the bus.

Everyone in the ever-growing crowd responded with a nervous chuckle. The third attacker let go of his grip on the girl, who then instantly sprinted to the awaiting bus. A state trooper emerged from the group of onlookers. Before the kidnapper had a chance to take a step toward Lamplighter, the trooper handcuffed the man to the picnic table.

The first guy stood up, then dropped back to his knees with his hands in the air at the command of the trooper. Backup arrived seconds later in the form of a sheriff's deputy who collected the smallest kidnapper. Lamplighter sat on the second man until a Shortsville village officer came to the scene and arrested the attacker.

Sheriff J.P. Cornell got there next. He was not duty at the time, but given the severity of the situation, he came from his home to supervise the situation.

Lamplighter had retreated to the bus to call his wife, Gloria, and inform her about what happened, and then came back out to give his statement. As he got off the bus, he observed the sheriff checking the necks of the girls and shaking their heads in the affirmative.

"Looks like you've gotten yourself into more trouble," said the sheriff when he spotted Lamplighter getting off the bus.

"I can't help it," replied Lamplighter. "Call me a Good Samaritan."

"With your luck, this is probably something a lot bigger than this incident," noted the sheriff. "So tell me what happened."

Lamplighter detailed the event in full, starting from when the woman started talking with him.

"Well, let me know if you think of anything else," said the sheriff. "You still has my card I assume?"

"Yeah," replied Lamplighter. "It's there somewhere."

The bus driver kept the bus late to make sure that everyone eventually made it back to Canandaigua. It arrived one-hour late.

"By the way," said the lady. "I like how you dress."

Lamplighter walked the six blocks home from the transfer station. He got home at 1 p.m.

Chapter 3

Lamplighter is on a quest for knowledge. This has two branches. He always had a thirst to know the details of Biblical history and prophecy, because of that; he has been a practicing Christian since high school graduation. Lamplighter also spent quite a bit of time delving into secular history and current events. Often the two interests intersected.

He has been an avid reader of the Bible since taking eighth-grade confirmation classes at his hometown United Methodist Church. Lamplighter finally accepts Christ as the savior after joining a study group in college. He also enjoyed watching Bible-based television programs, often ordering study guides. This year he has a goal of reading the entire Bible over the course of one year. Lamplighter's plan to accomplish this consists of reading five verses a day.

Upon getting home Monday afternoon, the first thing he did was read the day's five-verse passage. It was Isaiah chapters 20-24. The main point of the verses was to describe God's power by using examples of battles and natural disasters.

"He gave me the ability to win a battle against three people my size," thought Lamplighter.

His interest in prophecy led him to ponder chapter 22, verse 22: "And I will place on his shoulder the key of the house of David. He shall open, and none shall shut; and he shall shut, and none shall open."

Lamplighter understood this to foretell the coming of Christ. It made him think of how the Bible tells what is going to happen sometimes thousands of years in advance.

He remained dressed in his shirt and tie as he turned on the computer and sat down to work on the story. Lamplighter interviewed the Clifton Springs doctor because the M.D. was both battling cancer and treating cancer patients. He transcribed the recording of the interview.

"How does he do it?" he thought, recalling his mom's death from cancer more than 20 years ago.

His father, Ben, is also a cancer survivor and is still alive and residing in a senior housing complex in Lamplighter's hometown in Wisconsin. He decided to give his dad a call but got no answer.

"Must have gone out for a walk," Lamplighter thought as he got up to stretch.

He looked out the window to see Salvation Army Captain Morgan walking his poodle on the church property. Lamplighter liked to joke that he could jump out of his back window and land on Salvation Army property. He laughed as he turned on his radio and sat back down to work.

One place where his interests come together is the Gregg Matzek radio show. The host is on a crusade to topple what he sees as the coming one-world government. Matzek makes the case with how it relates to the first beast of Revelation. Lamplighter started to listen to his show after transcribing the interview.

Matzek was reciting patriotic quotes all week in honor of the upcoming July 4 weekend.

"Man is born free, but everywhere he is enslaved," said Matzek in reciting Rousseau.

"That's how I feel when I work at Wal-Mart," he thought.

He continued working on his stories by reading through some brochures and placing them in a folder. He then printed out the doctor's website. Lamplighter followed that by downloading the photos. He chose the best head shot of the subject, then selected one of the doctor working on a patient, who, surprisingly, approved to be in the photo.

"I'm glad she did that," thought Lamplighter. "A better story and a better photo."

Lamplighter finally changed out of his dress clothes.

"Not again," he said aloud with a sigh. "I just got this one."

He spotted a large rip on the back of the shirt. The Lamplighters were struggling financially, which left the wardrobe budget at a sparse level. The shirt was given to him by his coach, John Daniel, who has been helping him improve his discus throws.

Lamplighter thumped down on his bed.

"Looks like it's back to polo shirts for interviews," he thought.

Lamplighter got up and changed into T-shirt and pair of shorts. He set the alarm on his cell phone in anticipation of taking a nap and went back downstairs for a bite to eat - selecting a peanut butter and jelly sandwich on wheat toast - and watch the news. The local station was talking about upcoming construction on a downtown Rochester building.

"Another feature about which I am not interested," he thought as he looked for the remote.

Lamplighter searched the national channels for ideas he could try to sell the publishers of the publications for which he worked. The clients are the Victor News, a weekly newspaper that publishes his stories on local board meetings, Upstate Publishers, a company that uses his articles for its health, business and senior magazines; and Maranatha Monthly, a bi-monthly Christian newsletter.

"Maybe something on fishing in the area for the business magazine?" Lamplighter made a note to ask the editor about it.

He then flipped through the national cable news networks. Each one was focused on celebrity gossip.

"Why do people pay attention to that?" he said aloud with disgust.

Lamplighter settled on a few minutes of a Bible study show before rechecking the local station.

He got to the channel just in time to catch the weather report. It reminded him to take care of his other hobby.

Chapter 4

Lamplighter loved gardening, but living in a townhouse complex presented a small problem - no plot of land on which to grow his crops.

"I must admit," he said as he walked onto his back patio. "I did quite a good job of putting this together."

Lamplighter held his liquid fertilizer mix in his left hand and a pitcher of water in his right. He set the pitcher down to shut the door. He had left the vertical blinds open to the joy of his cat, TK, who loved to watch him through the glass. Gloria, and whatever other animals wandered out into the small concrete area, also offered an exciting experience for the pet.

"There you are," said Lamplighter has he looked down at the cat, who was staring up at him.

He kneeled down and wrapped on the glass to get one of her loud meows.

"Who's a good girl," he chuckled has the cat rubbed her declawed paw on the glass, matching that of her master's movement.

Lamplighter grinned and picked up both his pitcher and fertilizer. The cat's head followed him up. He smiled again as he heard another meow.

Lamplighter let out an enormous stress-relieving sigh of relief as he turned and headed toward his plants.

"Hard work, but quite a respite," thought Lamplighter before starting to water his plants.

Given the small space and small budget, he had to make do with ingenious contraptions from repurposed garbage.

He started to his immediate right. Lamplighter had set up two containers for Rutgers tomatoes. The plant needs depth for its roots to grow, so he kept large kitty litter containers, drilled holes in the bottom and filled them with dirt. Lamplighter created the lower level of a support cage by flipping the carrying handles up and attaching them together with zip ties. The rest of system included one dowel in each corner of dirt and intercrossing strings to which the taller plants could be tied.

For added support, the system was connected to a three-foot tall charcoal grill. Lamplighter took off the top and used that as his strawberry planter.

Finishing off that side was a similar two container system used for cherry tomatoes. Lamplighter finished off the water and went inside to refill the pitcher. He petted his cat on the head and went back outside, only to find Captain Morgan waiting for him on the other side of the fence that marked the border between the townhouses and the church.

"Good thing we don't have a drought like California," said Captain Morgan. "With their water rationing, you wouldn't be able to do that.

His poodle barked. Lamplighter turned to check on his cat, who only returned a curious-looking gesture.

"I thought of that while watching the news," replied Lamplighter, who was heading to the back area of the concrete.

This part of the patio was marked by a decorative bench. It wasn't strong enough to hold Don's weight, but it was perfect for five medium-sized clay pots that were holding his growing green peppers. Lamplighter continued to talk with the captain about the weather while watering the peppers.

"That is impressive how you figured out how to grow all of those crops in such a small space," said the captain.

"Oh, that reminds me," replied Lamplighter, who then suggested the church consider using some land for a garden.

Lamplighter gave the peppers fertilizer and water, then emptied the rest of the water on the tomatoes. He went back in for the third water pitcher fill, then came back out to find his neighbor Matt, firing up the grill.

"Howdy, neighbor," said Matt. "Saw you on the news again. You seem to have found yourself in trouble again."

"Already, yeesh," noted Lamplighter. "I'm in the news business and I am always impressed how quickly they get the scoop on stories."

"From anywhere, too," added Matt. "You can turn on the TV news here in Canandaigua and hear of wars in the Middle East, the weak economy in Europe, earthquakes in Japan, volcanoes in Indonesia, disease outbreaks in Africa and forest fires in the South. It's like hell is breaking out all over the place."

Lamplighter headed toward his third planting area. He made raised beds by taking an unused kitchen table and putting a heavy-duty tablecloth over it. Lamplighter improvised a basin by drilling holes into two long plastic drawers and placed them on top of the table. They were used for his ground-level vine plants - cucumbers in one and an experiment with spaghetti squash in the other.

"Add that to the Internet and you can find about just about anything," responded Lamplighter.

Lamplighter watered and fed the plants while his neighbor grilled hamburgers.

"I can't tell if events around the world are happening faster or we just hear more about them," said Matt.

"Probably both," laughed Lamplighter, who took a big sniff of the hamburgers.

"Want one?" asked Matt.

Lamplighter patted his belly.

"Sounds good, but no thanks," he said. "I just ate a good PB&J and I am headed in for a nap."

Lamplighter took his rest on the most comfortable chair in the living room.

Since he had his phone in his hand, Lamplighter decided to play the triples game with his wife. The game works when either he or Gloria would list three things, leaving the other to figure out why they are connected. They often used the game as a way to review their day.

"The kidnapping, my appetite and my new shirt," Don texted his wife. "I will just tell you the answer. Three things I've ruined today."

He tried to follow that by watching a film noir piece, but quickly fell asleep with the family cat on his belly. It was 2:30 p.m., nearly three hours before a city committee meeting to confirm the plans for its busiest workweek of the year.

Chapter 5

If Ken Knight were to list his favorite things, there would be a three-way tie. Knight enjoyed working on his computer, wearing his Absalom mask and conducting a meeting. On the first Monday of the month, he got to do all three at the same time.

Knight held two titles in the unnamed global Satanic cult. He was the captain of the Rochester region and major for New York State. It was tradition that the regional groups meet once a week at a time and place determined by the captain. The world group met once a year, with the most recent just nine days ago at a resort just outside of Canandaigua. The monthly meeting was his idea. One he called just because he likes to sit in meetings.

"A good month to all of you," he said in front of his computer screen.

The other regional captains - a college professor from Buffalo, banker working in Syracuse, sheriff in the Albany area and marketing executive from New York City - returned the greetings as the Absalom mask appeared on their screen. Per his new rules, the captains had to video conference together at 5 p.m.

"Welcome to the first of what will by many monthly meetings," continued Absalom. "First of all, I would like to congratulate all of you on your region's financial performance. Every one of you made a profit."

The four other attendees responded with various forms of "you're welcome."

"Plus with my money laundering and investment skills there is even a bit extra on that," said Absalom with a smile even though the captains couldn't see his face.

After the chuckles had subsided, Absalom continued with the agenda.

"Normally this would be the place where we would talk about the minutes from the last meeting," he said. "But since this is our first gathering, there aren't any."

An unintended moment of silence had reared before Absalom furthered the agenda by asking for a report from each of the captains. Being it so soon after their most recent gathering, none of the four had anything substantial to report, given that anyone in on the conference was already made aware of any local plans.

"OK now for the new business," stated Absalom. "I'm sure all of you by now have heard of a rash of child kidnapping in the Rochester area. Let me first assure you that they are not being done by members of my organization."

He stopped for a second to assume his favorite pose - leaning back with his hands interlocked in front of his face.

"I understand that some members of our group are into that sort of thing," he continued. "I, however, am not. I don't find it morally repugnant, but I'm an economic junky, and, well, the risk is just not worth the reward."

The statement reminded him of his investments. He paused to take a quick glance at a second computer on his desk for the most recent market reports.

"OK, since you are here," said the masked leader. "I will say that gold is up and I just sold some of our stake. The results not only bring a cool million to each of you, but to myself and to each of my task captains as well. The profits are being transferred into our Cayman Island accounts as we speak."

Applause erupted among the four other leaders.

"Now," he continued. "With that war we started in the Middle East, the oil prices continue to rise. We have made a substantial gain on that as well, but our analysis shows that it is going even higher, so our stake is going to stay there."

"Good move," replied the sheriff.

"One more thing," added Absalom. "Since each of us has shares in our organization's arms-dealing corporation, I am happy to report that shares are up too."

Again, there was more applause.

"Wait a second," he said, then quietly looked at the screen.

Nobody spoke during the one-minute study.

"However, that doesn't mean that we can't use the lessons learned from the most recent gathering to foster our group's agenda," Absalom added as he looked up. "Our friend from New York is going to explain what we are going to do."

The executive is part of a legacy family that is now in its ninth generation in the cult. He is also a member of the worldwide propaganda committee.

"Let me start with a quote from Plato," he said. "This and no other is the root from which a tyrant springs; when he first appears as a protector."

Every member of the group nodded.

"Well, let's make people come to us as a protector," he continued. "Each of us is in a position to bring people to us while . . . we . . . oh, shall we say, implement our agenda on them."

The executive's presentation continued for eight more minutes. Absalom then followed with instructions with how each member was going to execute that plan.

"OK," said Absalom. "Now let's recite our founding Bible verses."

The regional leads stood at attention.

"Genesis, chapter 3, verse 15," said Absalom.

"I will put enmity between you and the woman, and between your offspring and her offspring; he shall bruise your head, and you shall bruise his heel," they chanted.

Absalom raised his hands.

"John chapter 8, verse 44," he said.

"You are of your father the devil, and your will is to do your father's desires. He was a murderer from the beginning, and does not stand in the truth, because there is no truth in him. When he lies, he speaks out of his own character, for he is a liar and the father of lies," the leaders replied.

Absalom noted the final verse Revelation 13, verse 1.

"And I saw a beast rising out of the sea, with ten horns and seven heads, with ten diadems on its horns and blasphemous names on its heads."

The group took their seats

"Oh and one more thing before we close," noted Absalom. "I defeated Don Lamplighter in a game of chess this morning."

With that, he turned off his screen, took off his mask and took a drink of orange soda.

Chapter 6

Lamplighter enjoyed a good walk, and Monday evening was no exception. He had an eight-block trip to a meeting of his own. This one was all in fun. Lamplighter was headed to the city's event committee gathering. The group was going over final plans for this weekend's Independence Day celebration.

Lamplighter did his Wing Chun Sil Lin Tao and a cane fighting routine before heading out on his walk. Normally he would lift weights on Monday, but with the long walk ahead, he decided to use that as a substitute workout.

"I'm going to a meeting without my reporter's equipment," he said as left his townhouse. "This feels strange, but oddly relaxing."

He then paused, went back into the house to get at least his camera, notepad and pen.

"With my luck I never know when I need these," he said with a sigh to TK, who stared back in silence.

Lamplighter walked out of the townhouse parking lot, and got past it by one block before turning left down Beals Street. The next block was the first time he had to cross the street, over the busy, but poorly named, Pleasant Street, That was followed by a right-hand turn into a one-block jaunt. Two blocks after the next left, he hit Main Street.

The last time he was in this area was less than two weeks ago. Lamplighter had tried to convince a prostitute to attend a service at the Canandaigua Salvation Army Corps. His effort was thwarted by an enforcer for the local pimp. The goon was promptly arrested by Sheriff Cornell, who was following Lamplighter.

He stopped for a second and shook his head before continuing his trek, but failed to notice the shadowy man following him.

"Not-so-fond memories of this place," he thought.

Once on Main Street, it was two more blocks before reaching the office of the Chamber of Commerce. The Committee held its meeting in a conference room in the back.

His cell phone, which Lamplighter kept on vibrate mode, was going off just as he sat. It was Gloria.

"Just got into car. On my way home," she said.

Gloria had the family's one working car, a gold four-door Dodge Stratus, at the Dollar General Store in Newark, a 45-minute drive away. She held the rank of assistant manager and was often assigned out from the Canandaigua store to cover shifts in other communities.

"OK," replied Lamplighter. "Hey can you pick me up at the meeting?"

"Can do," she replied.

Lamplighter sipped on a glass of cold water supplied by the Chamber. Every one of the group's nine members gave a final report on what they had left to do before Saturday's big event.

The day featured four attractions. It started with a parade down Main Street to the city's waterfront park. There was a two-hour break before the park's gazebo was filled with various local musical acts beginning with a karaoke contest at 1 p.m. A lighted boat parade passed by the park at 9 p.m., immediately followed by a fireworks display, which was set off from a barge on the lake.

Lamplighter sat quietly until his report.

"First of all," he said. "I have four more posters left if anyone knows of a good place to put them up,"

Members of the group brainstormed suggestions until Lamplighter had the four locations selected.

He then previewed what he was planning on doing Saturday.

"OK, first I am going to the park to help set up tents and some chairs for the vendors and our headquarters," he said. "From there, I will head to the parade and make sure that the entries are in order."

"Are you sure you can do that with only one car?" chuckled Nancy Green, the group's chairman.

"Good question," replied Lamplighter. "I plan to drive to the park, then back to my townhouse. I will then drop my wife and the car off at her store, then walk to the staging area. That way she can have the car for work."

"You really have this worked out," noted Jill Berry, who was in charge of recruiting the musical acts.

"Well," laughed Lamplighter. "With the luck we have with our cars, we have a lot of experience."

The group got a good laugh.

"Then I will go home and nap," he added. "I will walk down to the park for a night shift in the city booth. Gloria will join me for the fireworks."

"Sounds you will have a busy day," said Paul Norton, the oldest member of the group, who was in charge of marketing.

"That is what I signed up to do," replied Lamplighter.

It actually wasn't for what he had signed up. Lamplighter was part of a neighborhood watch group that quickly fizzled out, at which time he left the organization. After a year, the people that remained with the watchers talked about getting new leadership. Lamplighter signed up again, only to have the city merge the walkers into a group called the City Pride Committee with the intent of having it act as a pseudo-recreation department that would organize picnics and other family-friendly events. The neighborhood watch section of the group was disbanded, but Lamplighter stayed on after deciding it would be a worthwhile way to contribute to the community.

Three more committee members gave their report before Green closed the meeting.

Gloria pulled up as Lamplighter and a few members were having an informal chat outside.

"See? We have this timed to a T," he said before kissing his wife.

She sat in the car smiling.

"Newark, Canandaigua, Honeoye," she said.

"Three stores where you worked in the past month," replied Lamplighter.

Gloria just nodded her head as they left the parking lot.

"OK, I got one," he said. "Canandaigua, Victor, Clifton Springs."

"That's easy," noted Gloria as she aimed the car down Pleasant Street. "Three places where you are going to work this week."

"True," said Lamplighter.

Gloria took the left-hand turn on Beals Street.

"The beach, home and someplace else fun," she said.

He gave two wrong guesses before getting the right answer.

'Three places where we plan to go on our day off tomorrow," he finally responded correctly.

The Lamplighters took a right onto Jefferson Avenue and a quick right into the townhouse parking lot.

"Snack, sleep and wait for you to come home," said Gloria.

'That sounds like a good plan for you for the rest of the night," he said.

Chapter 7

The Victor News desperately needed a copy for its next edition. The paper's niche is community news with the occasional national advice column and puzzle pages. For the local stories, it is entirely dependent on Lamplighter's coverage of town and village board meetings, or what other interesting information he can dig up around the village.

Tonight, he was headed to do a feature on gardening clubs at two churches.

"With this July 4 coming up, don't forget the lessons the founding fathers taught us about liberty," said Dr. Joe Hammill, one of Lamplighter's favorite companion shows for his regular freelance missions. "And don't forget we are in a spiritual battle to keep that liberty."

"Amen," thought Lamplighter just before pulling over to the side of the road at the first sight of a flashing red light.

A sheriff's department car raced past him.

"I wonder where that is going," he thought as his reporter instincts kicked in.

Lamplighter got back on the road. He got over the next hill and got his answer as that same deputy had pulled over a sports car on the side of the road.

"We must be vigilant in defending our liberty or it will be taken away from us," said the host.

"Well, that guy might have some taken away from him right now," laughed Lamplighter while looking at the sports car in his rearview mirror.

He continued north on Highway 332 and spotted an interesting billboard. Lamplighter recognized it right away as being from the Declaration of Independence

"We hold these truths to be self-evident, that all men are created equal, that they are endowed by their Creator with certain unalienable rights, that among these are life, liberty and the pursuit of happiness."

He didn't recognize who had rented the space, but had little time to look at the fine print of the sign before taking a right turn for his story target at the Farmington United Methodist Church.

A chance encounter at Wal-Mart led to a conversation with a member of that church, which had used some of the church's land to start a community garden.

"You weren't kidding about meeting here were you," asked the 60ish-aged woman who met him in the parking lot.

"I'm always looking for a story," he replied.

The two had met while Lamplighter was working as a part-time cashier at the Canandaigua Wal-Mart. He was working primarily in the garden center when the woman - Sarah Anderson - happened to come through his line. Once she explained why she was purchasing so many supplies, he explained about his writing jobs and took down her information for a future story. Anderson was more than happy to meet with him this Monday night to help promote her idea.

"This is a great story," she said "The churches in town, or at least the ones that have the available land, have come together to make what is essentially a giant garden."

The two walked around to the back of the church so Lamplighter could take photos of this part of the operation. There they met up with the church's pastor, the Reverend Michael Katt, and a group of teenaged boys who help maintain the garden.

"These serve a dual purpose," noted Katt. "We allow our parishioners a small plot to grow their own food and have an extra area set aside to feed the Victor community. Produce from that land is donated to the town food bank."

Lamplighter took out his recorder for interviews.

The Rev. Katt explained the Biblical example had inspired the project. He spoke of Christ's miracle of feeding the multitude of those that gathered to hear him, specifically reading Matthew 14, verses 14-21.

Lamplighter snapped photos of the field and the group of volunteers who maintained the lot.

Anderson noted that the church's plot was used for root vegetables. Lamplighter's second visit for the story was to a non-denominational church across the village. With less land to use, the congregation had set up an entirely different system. It employed raised beds with climbing vines and an automatic sprinkler system.

He was met there by a retired construction worker named Bill Holmes, who designed then supervised the church's volunteers in building the garden system. Being interested in gardening, Lamplighter was fascinated by the techniques.

"This is an impressive system," he told Holmes. "Show me how it works."

Holmes was reluctant to appear in the photos, instead allowing the volunteers to demonstrate the project for Lamplighter's lens.

Lamplighter finished the interviews and left eager to get home and finish the story. The route he took sent him past the railroad track where he rescued the infant. He thought about it until he was interrupted by another set of flashing lights. He pulled over to allow it to pass. This time it was an ambulance. The reporter in him compelled him to follow. Lamplighter stopped just before the right-hand turn to allow a sheriff's vehicle to get in front of him.

"What is the big rush?" he wondered as he got onto Brace Road.

The caravan drove to the municipal park.

"OK, this is not going to turn out well," he thought as he got his equipment out for a potential story.

Lamplighter noted two sheriff vehicles, one state trooper, the ambulance, the volunteer fire department with its dive team and some workers from the village department of public works. He felt like he was back in Clifton Springs as Sheriff Cornell approached.

"How did you get here so fast?" asked Cornell.

"I was in town on another story and followed a deputy here," replied Lamplighter. "So what's going on?"

"I can't comment right now unless it is off the record," noted Sheriff Cornell.

"Well, my deadline is not until Sunday anyway," replied Lamplighter.

"A good point," sighed Sheriff Cornell with a sigh. "The workers here were building on the berm when they noticed a body floating in the pond."

Lamplighter snapped a picture of a diver getting into the water.

"Any idea who it was?" asked Lamplighter.

"All we know is that it was a young girl and she was already dead," said Sheriff Cornell. "Please note that we just found her so there is no ID, but she appeared to be between seven and ten years old."

"So is it part of the recent rash of missing young children?" asked Lamplighter.

"We just found her, so we haven't even started an investigation yet," noted Sheriff Cornell. "But there is evidence that she is possibly connected to some of the other crimes."

Lamplighter asked what that evidence was. Sheriff Cornell refused to answer specifically.

"Well this just happened in Victor," said Lamplighter. "So now it is my investigation too."

Lamplighter texted both his wife and his editor to explain what was happening. He then conducted interviews, or what served for interviews so early in the investigation. Lamplighter took photographs and stayed until the ambulance left the park.

"On the way home," he said in a message to his wife just after starting his car.

Lamplighter relaxed by listening to soft gospel music for the 20-minute drive home. He and Gloria enjoyed a meal of homemade chicken Parmesan, and he went upstairs to the spare room in the townhouse. He downloaded all of his photos and transcribed his recordings from both the gardens and the dead child stories.

"Got those in the computer," he said to Gloria, who was popping popcorn.

Later, the Lamplighters cuddled on the love seat and watched two movies.

When they can, the Lamplighters do their nightly Bible study together. The Bible they use is a condensed version that included just the New Testament and the books of Psalms and Proverbs. They trade nights picking verses and do so by randomly by flipping the pages with their thumbs and reading where they felt like they needed to stop. Tonight he ended in James chapter 3. The passage spoke on the differences between Earthly wisdom and wisdom from God.

They went to bed together at midnight and discussed verse 17 "But the wisdom from above is first pure, then peaceable, gentle, open to reason, full of mercy and good fruits, impartial and sincere."

They agreed that it was easier said than done.

Lamplighter rubbed Gloria's back until she fell asleep. He stayed up thinking about the day's events and what it meant for the future.

"It looks like my week just got a whole lot busier," he whispered.

Chapter 8

"Man, I love sitting in meeting," said Absalom as he stretched out and cracked his knuckles.

"Wow," grumbled Madam Stephanie. "You truly are evil. No other way you could enjoy this."

Absalom, as he does every Monday night, is leading the meeting of his captains. The group gets together in a room at a downtown nightclub that is now owned by a dummy corporation that Absalom set up just for the property.

"My second one today," he replied while scanning the gathering from his head-of-the-table vantage point. "If I had my way there would be even more, but I ran out of groups to run."

The seven captains all chuckled.

"So as usual, I will start," he said. "I take it you all recovered from our summer solstice party?"

His leaders nodded in agreement.

"Well I can tell you that all the notes I have received from honored guests have been positive," Absalom continued. "I assure that all of you are going to get a generous bonus for this. Each one has been transferred to your secret bank accounts."

Absalom took a lap around the room, sharing a fist bump with each member before retaking his seat.

"Also it looks like our monthly financials are going well thanks to all of your efforts," he continued. "We are doing a great job of bilking the Rochester area of all of its worth."

"My girls are finding out that there is a lot to be taken," noted Madam Stephanie, who ran the group's prostitution ring.

Absalom nodded at her as a signal to begin her report.

"The money is rolling in as our women are, can I say, rolling around," she said. "Don Lamplighter set us back a bit in Canandaigua, but no matter. We are taking over the other suburbs quite well."

Absalom looked at her again.

"Our fearless leader's brilliant idea to get into the Internet for hookups has made our scheduling rather easy," she added as she sat back in her chair. "And rather more profitable, too."

Absalom then looked at Steve, who was a city council member and served as the group's political insider

"Well, I am on my way to a fundraiser so I have to make this quick," said the councilman. "I know that I bore you with this stuff, but here we go anyway. We have a judge that is leading in the polls for the November election and the zoning change for our real estate investment is going to go through."

Steve rushed through the door, leaving the floor for Vic, who was in private security and provided the muscle.

"Not much to say other than to thank you for your help at the solstice," he quipped. "Oh, yeah. We got a private security contract for the new office building downtown."

Absalom then gave the floor to Julius, who was in charge of the drug trade.

"Did you see that drug bust on the news?" he asked. "One of our competitors that I set up. Now we control all of the west side."

The group clapped.

"Speaking of the west side," chirped in Gabrielle the grifter. "I am running a blackmail scheme on the pastor in Greece that was campaigning against our adult video store. He will shut up."

That brought the conversation to Alexander, who was in control of a theft scheme.

"Those guys that Lamplighter caught in Canandaigua were killed in jail so they won't be talking," he said. "There are new stores opening soon in Victor and Macedon and we have our scouts already working on the inside."

Absalom stood up and took another lap around the table.

"Our colleague from New York has put together a plan that the country is going to use to form our global control grid," he stated as he got to his chair, but didn't sit down. "Part of what we want to do is put and RFID chip into everyone in the planet."

"I thought that was way off in the future," said Vic.

Absalom pointed at him.

"Thank you for bringing that up," said the leader as he finally took his seat. "It was supposed to be that way, however, we were so successful convincing people to put them in pets that we are going to advance our idea ahead a bit."

He pulled out a notebook.

"Our marketer started his meeting with a quote from Plato, but I have a better one," Absalom said as he ruffled through the pages. "This one is from the mayor of Chicago. 'You never let a serious crisis go to waste. And what I mean by that is an opportunity to do things you think you could not do before.'"

Madame Stephanie raised her hand.

"I think I can answer that for you," replied Absalom. "You know those eight missing kids that are all over the news this week. We had nothing to do with that, but parents are scared out of their minds."

Absalom interlocked his fingers and grinned.

"So scared that they are going to be convinced to put chips in their children," he said. "And Ken

Knight is going to help them do that."

Absalom put a video of the morning's conference on a projection screen for all of his captains.

"Remember that I am deleting this one after we show it so pay attention," he said. I have a quiz later."

His captains laughed. After the viewing, he further explained the plan.

"As Madame Stephanie so graciously explained, we are going to take advantage of the missing children," he said. "Yes, our goal is to get everyone in the world chipped so our organization can keep track of everybody."

All of the captains nodded.

"But if we try to force people to do it, they will fight back," he said. "This way we will have people lining up for it and they will have no idea what is really happening to them."

Chapter 9

The Lamplighters had been looking forward to this day for three weeks. Lamplighter noticed the quirk in scheduling that left him a Tuesday with no meeting to cover the night before. This meant that he would not spend the day drudging through pages and pages of notes and agendas while trying to craft a detailed, yet interesting, article.

To get ready for the day, he woke himself up at 11:30 a.m. He started off with his morning devotional. Today he was on Isaiah 25-29. The verses continued the course of God's power. He drew strength from Chapter 26, verse 4: "Trust ye in Jehovah forever; for in Jehovah, even Jehovah, is an everlasting rock."

He completed the back patio plant-watering routine, and then finished his Sil Lin Tao and cane-fighting practice. Lamplighter followed that by watching the news for any updates on either Monday morning's run-in with kidnappers or Monday night's incident in the Victor Park. The noon news on his favorite local channel covered both events, but neither included information that he already didn't know.

"I must have had quite a day if my two news stories take precedence over the national news," he thought.

Lamplighter played catch with a baseball-sized rubber ball as he contemplated the development.

"But they didn't find anything else more than I already know," he said to the cat, who had sat by his feet.

He put the ball down and picked the cat up for nap time. Lamplighter was scratching the cat's neck when he had another thought.

"Either their reporters didn't ask any questions or they did and the sheriff didn't respond on the record to them either," he added. "But how did they know in the first place since they weren't even there?"

He went back up to his office and checked his email. There was a press release regarding the Victor scene. It was so basic that it contained nothing more than the information that the news channel reported.

"Tight lipped," he said. "This means it's something big. I have to find out what."

Gloria's alarm clock blared.

"But the story isn't due until Sunday," he thought. "And I have a promise to keep with my wife."

Being the acting manager of the Canandaigua Dollar General store left Gloria in a position where she could schedule herself her own day off. The decision to pick today was easy.

Gloria awoke at 12:30 p.m. to feed the cat and get the towels and other beach supplies ready.

The pair had some work to do on the trip.

"About ready to go?" she asked at the pre-decided 1 p.m. departure time.

"Looking forward to it," replied her husband, who appeared dressed for the occasion in his swimsuit with his cane in one hand and beach towel in the other.

As per the event committee meeting, Lamplighter selected locations for the four remaining July 4 event posters. He had already hit up the few stores in the city, leaving only the Salvation Army store downtown, the laundromat hidden in a strip mall along highways 5 and 20 in the south side of town, a bulletin board at the bus transfer area and a sound-off wall at the main entrance to Finger Lakes Community College.

They were accompanied on the trip by the Gregg Matzek radio show. The host and a guest were discussing the economy. Lamplighter held a college degree in economics and found the discussion interesting.

Gloria drove the whole trip. She pulled the couple's sedan into the last spot in the beach area's 20-vehicle capacity lot. The only entrance to the beach was through a shelter that included locker rooms and a turnstile that served as the barrier to the main deck. The Lamplighters wore their residence passes on their wrists so the lifeguard let them pass without even a glance.

"You certainly like to carry things," remarked Gloria as she watched her husband successfully trek to an open spot in the grass while carrying two chaise lounges in his left hand.

"I find it fun," he said even though he walked with the use of his ever-present cane in his right hand.

The Lamplighters found a good spot and claimed it by setting down the chairs and towels. Lamplighter came dressed to go right in the water. Gloria wore her suit underneath a T-shirt and pair of shorts.

"IGA, McDonald's, City Pier," said Gloria as they held hands on their way to lake.

"I was thinking the same thing," he replied. "Places we could to go get ice cream after this."

Lamplighter walked right into Canandaigua Lake, cane and all. He and Gloria set a course for the deepest part of the roped-off designated swimming area. He hooked his cane on the rope as he swam around while Gloria enjoyed digging holes with her feet. He then demonstrated how he could stand on his hands. Gloria tested herself to see how long she could hold her breath underwater.

They played around for a half hour before heading for shore. They both showered the beach sand off and took their seats to dry off before getting back into the car.

Lamplighter laughed as he removed the rubber stopper from the end of his cane to let the water drain.

"You know what you should try next time?" asked Gloria. "Keep that end on and cover up the holes. You could use it as a snorkel."

He examined the cane. It was metal. The handle was supposed to have a fabric loop on the grip end, but it fell out while being used as a cat toy. The middle featured holes to hold a metal pin. The placement of the pin determined the length of the cane.

"Actually that will work," he said.

The Lamplighters packed up. They got into the car just as Matzek was closing his show with another message from the country's founding fathers - General Nathanael Greene. He related it to his frustration getting information out against political power

"We fight, get beat, rise and fight again."

The Lamplighters chose to get their ice cream at City Pier, an ice cream store that occupies a small store on the pier, in order to watch the ducks gather along the rocky breakwater.

"I would say this has been a fantastic afternoon," said Lamplighter as he leaned in for a kiss.

Chapter 10

Allan Buchanon liked to sit on the swing in the farthest west section of Lakeshore Park. He has been scouting this location for a couple of weeks, just waiting for another phone call.

Buchanon is 37 years old, single, unemployed and a fan of toy poodles. It was through a Rochester-area club of poodle owners where he made the connection that could get him some money.

"I got one for you," said the voice on the other end of his pre-paid cell phone.

Buchanon looked around to make sure that nobody was watching, or at least listening.

"Go ahead," he replied.

He listened as his contact described the order. Buchanon never wrote down the information, but committed it to memory so to not leave a paper trail in case he got caught.

"I'll find you a good one," he said.

Buchanon stood up, stretched and took a quick look at the landscape and headed east for a walk around the park.

One popular feature of Lakeshore Park is that dogs are allowed. Buchanon and his poodle, Max, took their normal route along the lakeshore path. After passing several other swings, the two came to the gazebo where Lamplighter and his committee will host the bands for Saturday's July 4 celebration.

"I can't wait for the fireworks," he said as he bent down to pat Max on the head.

The back of the gazebo includes a deck that juts out over the lake. A few yards out was a fountain that shot lake water into various timed spray formations. Buchanon took pictures as he took note of the crowd that gathered to watch the show.

Max led the way as they left the gazebo and headed to the playground. Buchanon took note of several kids pointing at his dog as they walked by.

"Just as I want them to do," he thought with a grin.

Buchanon's dog has been getting him attention ever since he adopted him from the local pound five years ago. He joined a club for poodle owners. At one of these meetings, he befriended a

fellow Army veteran. After Buchanon had lost his job when the car part manufacturing company he worked for took operations from Canandaigua to Mexico, he sought help from his new friend.

His Army buddy then introduced him to the world of pedophilia. Although Buchanon doesn't participate in the sex acts, he makes money from the trade by kidnapping children for delivery to the leader, who then took them to members of his friend's group.

Buchanon learned how to use Max as a prop to lure in children. He was getting proficient at his trade and making enough money to offset the difference between his unemployment checks and his debts.

The path brought the two along the parking lot where the vendors will be set up Saturday. It was followed by the beach.

"Who is that idiot trying to walk in the water with his cane?" he thought before moving onto the concession stand, pavilion and small-craft launch site.

The next stop was an ice cream shop that occupied the first floor of a conference center. Buchanon tied up Max and went in to get a soft-serve twist cone to use as yet another prop.

"According to a study I read, eating this makes one look approachable," he thought as he walked out the door. "Let's hope it works."

Just as he wanted. A family had stopped to pet Max, who had definitely enjoyed the attention.

"Have you been a good boy?" he said as he again stooped to pat his pet.

Max stood on his hind legs to the delight of the crowd. Buchanon had conversations about the dog with a young woman who was walking with what he found out was a seven-year-old boy. He was blonde, just like his contact's client ordered.

Buchanon learned that they were going to play on the slides for a while. He avoided suspicion by continuing east, away from the playground. The next landmark was the sternwheeler that brought tourists on nightly dinner cruises. After that was another section of the park, that mirrored the peaceful part of the far west side.

"It looks like the study was somewhat right," he thought.

Buchanon needed to rush to finish his melting cone before the hot weather caused a mess.

"A mess does not attract the right kind of attention," he thought, quickening the pace of his ice cream consumption. "I need to get to the playground in time to make my money."

He tried to save time by walking and eating the cone at the same time, but that made it harder to keep clean and the small napkin that comes with the treat was starting to become saturated with melt. Buchanon sat on a swing just like his favorite on the other side of the park to finish the ice cream.

He examined his hands before again petting Max.

"Are you ready to go to work?" he asked as Max leaped.

Buchanon made contact with the boy and his mother. A short time into the conversation, he noted that he was going to get Max some water. The boy came along with him.

The water and dish were strategically placed on the far end of the car, which was parked in a spot in the street so a line of hedges blocked the view from the playground.

"Can you please go in and get them?" he asked of his prey.

As soon as he got in the car, Buchanon shut the door. He then quickly placed Max in the front passenger seat, got into the driver's seat and took off.

"Easier than I thought it would be," he thought as he headed to the rendezvous point with his Army buddy.

"I filled your order," he said as he pulled into a small park along the east side of Canandaigua Lake. "I will meet you as planned."

Chapter 11

"I don't have children of my own, but I realize that they are our most important resource," said Ken Knight from the podium in front of one of his banks. "The future of mankind depends on the future of our children."

Knight looked out at the crowd that gathered in for one of his rare press conferences. It was exactly as he wanted. All three of Rochester's national television affiliates were there, as well as the local 24-hour news channel. The 4 p.m. event was getting all of the attention he wanted.

"As you can tell from my previous donations, my foundation has hundreds of thousands of dollars to both educate and protect our children," he added.

Knight continued his mental survey of the crowd. After mergers and business failings, just two newspaper organizations remained to cover Rochester. Both of them had a reporter and photographer on the scene.

He then introduced the members of his foundation. The board consisted of an all-star collection of people who deal with Rochester's youth on a daily basis. Starting from his left, Knight introduced two local pastors, one public school principal, one private school principal, the police chief, education professors from two area colleges, the director of the local children's museum, a pediatrician, and an owner of a chain of kids-oriented clothing stores. Knight then introduced himself as the chairman of the group.

"We have worked hard to find a solution to the problems of the youth in the Rochester area," he said.

All seven of Knight's captains were trained to stay away from such events to lessen the possibility of anyone making connections between members of his criminal leadership council. Madam Stephanie and Gabrielle both watched from Knight's house on posh East Avenue.

"For a shy computer-guy introvert he looks like a natural at a press conference," noted Gabrielle. "How did you coach him up so well?"

"I told him to think about it as if he is directing a meeting," laughed Madame Stephanie as she took a sip of champagne.

"That will work," replied Gabrielle.

Knight gave a third look out at the media in front gathered by his podium. He counted four radio reporters as well.

"The board and I are deeply troubled by the events of the past couple of weeks," he continued. "News reports have eight children gone missing in the Rochester area. This is terrible. I have just

received word that a ninth has reportedly been abducted in Canandaigua. Not to mention the three that were saved from a Clifton Springs Park Monday morning."

Wine was the beverage of choice of Gabrielle. She took a sip, then let out a sigh of relief.

"Looks like he decided to leave out Lamplighter," she said.

"That was our consensus," noted Madame Stephanie. "No sense in letting our enemies more positive attention."

After taking a quick nap, Lamplighter tuned into the press conference just after the last comment. He flipped on the television, which was left on the 24-hour news channel. A live feed of the press conference was trumping the regularly scheduled weekly interview with a roundtable of doctors.

"These abductions show that the world is getting to be a more dangerous place," continued Knight. "The foundation and I want to make sure that law enforcement has the tools to both prevent future abductions and track children if they are the victim of the awful crime of abduction."

The board members nodded in agreement.

"That is why we are sponsoring an effort to get all children in the Rochester area implanted with RFID chips," he said. "This will be a valuable tool to help the outstanding law enforcement officials in our community quickly find any children reported missing."

Knight paused for applause from the members of the public that gathered on the sidewalk just to observe the display. The break gave the TV cameras time to pan through the law enforcement personnel in attendance.

"Once the criminals in our area know that our kids are protected by both the chip and the dedicated men and women that you see here," he added, "It will deter them from trying to harm that resource."

"Just like Gregg Matzek said," thought Lamplighter. "I wondered what this guy was up to."

Knight again waited for the applause to die down.

"The chips will be given to children only after getting parental permission," added Knight. "All tags will be free of charge with the procedure performed by Dr. Black's clinic."

Knight then motioned for Dr. Black to come to the podium.

"If you will excuse me," said Knight. "I am leaving the rest of the conference in the capable hands of Dr. Black. A packet of information outlining the details of the program will be given to every member of the media after this press conference."

Knight's cell phone started to vibrate as he immediately sneaked back into his office.

The first text message was from Madame Stephanie.

"Brilliant. You played the hero, then left the details to others."

Another message quickly popped up.

"Perfect, once this test is over we will take this statewide," said the marketing guru from New York City. "Then the country, then the world."

Lamplighter thought of his study of Revelation Chapter 13 verses 16 and 17: "And he causeth all, both small and great, rich and poor, free and bond to receive a mark in their right hand, or in their foreheads. And that no man might buy or sell save he that had the mark, or the name of the beast, or the number of his name."

"Could this be the start of that?" he wondered. "It would be a great way to trick people into getting something like that."

Chapter 12

Lamplighter's work was interrupted by a ringing doorbell.

"It's for you!" shouted Gloria up to her husband from the first floor of their townhouse.

"Actually we are here to see both of you," said Sheriff Cornell.

Everyone took a seat in the Lamplighters' small living room. The scene was a reminder of one just two Tuesdays ago when the sheriff and Lamplighters discussed the rescue of a baby from a hospital. The difference this time is the presence of Canandaigua detective Tom Ryne.

Lamplighter made sure to save his work on the church garden story before coming down the stairs.

"Be there in a second," he replied, then turned off the radio's gospel music show.

Gloria was cooking dinner - her favorite - a homemade lasagna that she not only made for herself and her husband, but also shared with her co-workers and neighbors. While she was cooking, Lamplighter spent the time on his articles. He planned to stop for the day after dining with his wife.

He enjoyed the enticing smell of the now-in-the-oven supper as he walked down the stairs, eager, but dreading who was calling on the Lamplighters this time.

"Mr. Lamplighter, nice to finally meet you," said Det. Ryne as the two shook hands. "I wish it was under better circumstances."

The four took their seats, with the Lamplighters next to each other on the love seat and Sheriff Cornell across from them on the rocking chair. Det. Ryne on sat a high-back chair that was against a third wall.

"Det. Ryne and I are here because of the child kidnappings in the area," stated Cornell. "But I bet the two of you have already figured that out."

Both Lamplighters just nodded.

"I'm also sure that you are aware that one more child has gone missing," added Det. Ryne

"Yes, the news said that a young boy was reportedly taken from Lakeshore Park," said Lamplighter.

"Well here's the thing," noted Det. Ryne. "Your names were on the list of people that used their beach pass at the time when the child was taken."

"I was wondering about that," said Gloria. "Was it from that part of the park?"

Det. Ryne recalled the details of the incident.

"We are interviewing everyone who used their pass at that time," replied Det. Ryne. "What did you see?"

"Well," responded Lamplighter. "I swim with my glasses off so all I can see is Gloria's face."

Gloria adjusted her hair as she blushed.

"We were so far out in the water that I didn't see anything either," said Gloria. "Once we got out, we cleaned off and looked out at the water so if it happened like you said it did, it would have been behind us."

Sheriff Cornell and Det. Ryne looked at each other and nodded. Cornell pulled out a police artist's sketch of Allan Buchanon.

"Did you see anyone that looked like this?" he asked, adding that he might have been walking a poodle.

The Lamplighters both took a look and noted that the face did not look familiar to them.

"Well then, Don," said Sheriff Cornell as he leaned forward in the chair. "The reason we are both here is because we are both on a task force created to solve these kidnappings."

Det. Ryne leaned forward as well.

"You were at the scene in Victor and the event in Clifton Springs," he said. "Did you see anyone that looked like the drawing at either of those locations?"

Lamplighter reviewed what he saw at each scene. In neither place did he recall seeing a person that looked like the sketch. He paused.

"Can I reason from what you asked that you have evidence that the missing children cases are related in some way?" asked Lamplighter.

Det. Ryne and Sheriff Cornell looked at each other.

"You know how it is on TV," replied Sheriff Cornell. "We always withhold evidence from the media. Something that would both identify the perpetrators and scare them away."

Lamplighter sat quietly again. He knew that Sheriff Cornell had just told them the answer for which he was looking.

"And since one of the bodies was found in Victor it puts the investigation into my coverage territory," said Lamplighter. "That makes me a member of the media. This means you are not going to tell me."

Sheriff Cornell sat back in his chair.

"You catch on quickly." He stood as he handed a copy of the sketch to Gloria. "If either of you think of anything, give us a call."

Both members of law enforcement put on their hats and headed for the door.

"So would you gentlemen like any lasagna?" said Lamplighter. "Gloria has a fantastic recipe and made a big batch of it."

"No thanks," replied Sheriff Cornell. "We actually ate right before we got here."

'That's OK," said Gloria as she hugged her husband's arm. "More for us."

Lamplighter went back up to the spare room that he used as his writing office. He finished the rough draft of the garden story, then completed a version of the article about the doctor from Clifton Springs.

The Lamplighters helped themselves to their portions of the meal while discussing the case.

For the couple's nightly devotional, Lamplighter took his turn to randomly select from the condensed Bible. Tonight, his thumb landed on Romans, chapter 9. The Lamplighters read the next five chapters. The passages broached two topics that they were discussing: Who gets into heaven and how a Christian should act. The Lamplighters had been discussing what they are looking for in a church since they have yet to find one that fit all of their requirements. They

both noted chapter 10, verse 4: "For Christ is the end of the law for righteousness to everyone who believes."

They went to bed together at 1 a.m.

"Clifton Springs, Wal-Mart and the hospital," he said.

"Any easy one," she replied. "Places in the county where you rescued a kid."

There was a one-minute pause before Gloria added a quiz of her own.

"Lasagna, shepherd's pie, crostini sandwiches," said Gloria.

Lamplighter was stumped, but finally got it correct after several guesses.

"The last three meals you made on our days off," he said.

"Correct," replied Gloria.

He leaned over and kissed her

"And great meals they were."

Chapter 13

"Huzzah to the hero," said Mitch the bus driver as Lamplighter transferred to his bus at 12:25 Wednesday afternoon.

"I wish I wasn't" replied Lamplighter as he took his traditional seat behind the driver.

"Well, somebody had to save them," noted Mitch as other passengers started to board.

"My point is that it means that there is a problem to solve in the first place," said Lamplighter. "If we didn't have child molesters in the first place, there would be no need to save the kids from them."

Buses were required to stay at the transfer point in downtown Canandaigua until at least 12:30 p.m. Mitch, who like Lamplighter is a devout Christian, was just about to close the door when he turned back to Lamplighter.

"I call it divine intervention," he said. "Be glad that God put somebody with your willingness to help on the bus at that exact time."

Lamplighter quietly pondered the point, then he reflected on the couple's transportation plan.

Gloria's day started at 8 a.m. Lamplighter's shift at the Wal-Mart garden center started at 2 p.m. Their simple plan for the day was to have Gloria use that car all day while Lamplighter took the bus to his shift. He made sure to water his plants, practice his fighting techniques and have a filling breakfast.

Lamplighter's morning Bible study continued in Isaiah. For Wednesday, it was chapters 30-34. The passages regarded God's judgment on the nations. Lamplighter compared them to the actions of people in his time. One verse in particular, chapter 32, verse 7, he related to Knight. "The instruments also of the schemer are evil; he deviseth devices to destroy the poor with lying words even when the needy speaketh right."

Mitch's words reminded him of the morning study. The route for Lamplighter's bus went right past Gloria's store. He gave a wave as it went by.

"But what about the girl that was found in the Victor Park on Monday?" asked Lamplighter. "Why wasn't I, or anybody else for that matter, there for her?"

"You were there too?" questioned Mitch.

"Yeah I was in the village on a story about churches using their property for gardens," responded Lamplighter. "I found out by following the ambulance and sheriff's cars."

The bus took a left-hand turn to head toward an area of Canandaigua noted for its medical facilities.

"You know what," continued Lamplighter. "I was also at Lakeshore Park when the child went missing yesterday."

"What did you see?" said Mitch as the bus pulled into an eye care facility.

"Funny that you ask me while we are here in this parking lot," responded Lamplighter. "Because you know what I saw? Nothing. I take my glasses off when I am in the water and I had my back to the park later. As the saying goes, I don't have eyes in the back of my head."

The next stop was an outbuilding that housed the hospital's billing department. Lamplighter looked down at the scar he got from helping at a car vs. train accident two weeks ago. He was silent as he wondered how he was going to pay the bill without health insurance.

"Another drawback of getting laid off," he thought. "The place where I work provides it, but I can't afford that and rent, and a car payment, and food, and car insurance and, well, everything else."

He rubbed his arm. Another passenger, who worked in the men's clothing department at Wal-Mart, took notice.

"Arm bothering you?" she asked.

"No," replied Lamplighter. "Everything around it is."

The bus approached the same hospital where Lamplighter rescued the baby and had the stitches put into his arm from the gash he suffered at the train wreck.

"I heard about you from the news," she said. "Anything I could do to help?"

"I could use another dress shirt," laughed Lamplighter.

Mitch drove the bus to the hospital, nursing home and dentist office complexes.

"This did bring you into the investigation?" she asked

"Well yeah," responded Lamplighter. "Both as a writer and as a witness."

The bus then pulled over next to an apartment complex.

"So you can stop other kids from being taken by solving the case, or at least help the police crack it," noted Mitch. "Just like you did with the woman who was murdered."

"I'm already on it," said Lamplighter. "In fact, I talked to the sheriff and a Canandaigua detective last night."

"What did you learn?" asked Mitch as he turned the bus onto the south side of Main Street.

"They seemed to think that all of the missing children are somehow connected," replied Lamplighter. "I know what happened in three of the cases. I am going to start from there."

They both stayed silent for several more stops. Lamplighter observed the face of each new rider with a futile hope that one of them would match the man in the sketch and he could end the case right then.

The bus traveled to a stop in a strip mall and to the Wegman's grocery store.

It then hit another strip mall before turning south to make a visit to the front entrance of the Finger Lakes Community College. Lamplighter's departure point was next.

"He had a car there," said Lamplighter.

"I don't follow," replied Mitch.

"Think about it," said Lamplighter. "The abduction yesterday featured a car, but the victims from Monday morning traveled by bus and the one from Monday night. There are no motor vehicles allowed in the park, so he had to walk a bit to drop the body off."

"So that makes the connection harder to spot," said Mitch.

"Yeah it does," sighed Lamplighter as he sat back in his seat. "Yeah it does."

Lamplighter saluted Mitch as he left the bus and headed into Wal-Mart.

"Busy day I see," said Mike, the greeter.

"Sad," noted Lamplighter. "I come to Wal-Mart and it's actually a stress relief."

The bus system puts him at the store 45 minutes before the start of his shift. Lamplighter poured a cup of coffee and collected some newspapers to see what they had to say about the children.

While he was reading, the same shadowy figure got off the bus and slipped into an awaiting car.

Chapter 14

A black limousine pulled up in front of Dr. Black's office as a crowd immediately surrounded the vehicle.

"Time for phase two," said Absalom as he removed his mask to take the form of Ken Knight.

Vic's private security team divided the crowd into two camps - one eagerly awaiting the RFID chip and a smaller number protesting the event.

"We are showing the arrival of Ken Knight," said the young female reporter from the 24-hour news channel. "We are here at 3 p.m., after a slight delay in getting the chips here from their manufacturing plant in Texas. Knight is here to be the first one to get implanted."

A bodyguard opened the door for Knight. He was immediately cheered by those who saw his gesture as a way to save their children and heckled by the nine-person group of protesters who saw this as another step in a global takeover.

The security team had made a path through the crowd. Vic's top lieutenant, a man, simply known as Garfield, led the way as Knight and a woman from a public relations firm approached the podium.

"Thank you all again for coming here on such short notice," said Knight once the crowd had settled down. "I understand that some of you have concerns about the motives of my plan to help the children of Rochester."

Vic's security team formed a tight circle around Knight and members of the media as the crowd again erupted in shouting matches. Since the clinic was on private property, it was allowed it to make a rule forbidding protest signs.

City police arrived to help with crowd control. Both sides quieted down upon their arrival.

"I assure that I only have the interests of our children at heart," continued Knight. "With this new technology we can now easily find children that are either lost or heaven forbid, kidnaped."

Madame Stephanie and Gabrielle again watched from Knight's mansion.

"Even better than last night," said Stephanie.

"That is from your coaching, my dear friend," replied Gabrielle, again congratulating her fellow captain on her instructions.

A nurse and secretary from Dr. Black's office came out to carry out the lottery system. Each parent who wanted the RFID chip implanted in their children signed up upon arrival. The next step was to assign a number to each candidate. A physician's assistant was responsible for drawing the numbers.

Knight explained the procedure from the podium.

"I apologize that there are not enough chips to satisfy all of your needs," noted Knight. "I assure you that more shipments have been ordered, and I will notify the media when they arrive."

Health magazine editor Dale Gray watched the scene with quite a bit of interest. He rushed to his computer to send an urgent email.

"This is something we need to cover," he typed in an email to Lamplighter. "See if you can get a story about this RFID thing for our next issue. Please get both sides of the issue. It is a Sunday deadline, same as your doctor story."

A young mother shouted from the waiting line.

"Then why are you getting one?" was the query.

"Thank you for asking," responded Knight. "Speaking of assurance, there are people here today who don't trust these things. By taking one myself, I am proving to them that they are safe."

Knight then stood on his tiptoes.

"And I am not much bigger than a kid anyway," he said as members of the media chuckled.

"An impromptu joke?" remarked a curious Gabrielle. "I wonder who taught him that."

Madame Stephanie just smiled.

Knight then pointed at the television reporter.

"And you are coming with me," he said. "Please refer to my prepared statement for any questions."

With that, Knight, Vic's hand-picked security and the reporter headed into the building.

Nobody said a word as the entourage headed for Dr. Black's second-story office. The receptionist greeted them and handed Knight the requisite forms.

"Here you go sir," she said. "Standard procedure."

Knight completed the forms, again without saying a word. He and Dr. Black shook hands for the camera before Knight sat on the paper-covered exam table. The doctor, who was specially trained in the RFID injection procedure, pulled out the needle. Knight flinched.

"Sorry," he said with a red face. "I'm still afraid of those."

The reporter recorded the entire procedure. Knight flinched again as the needle was put into his arm.

"Now I have something else to show you," said Knight as he held out his arm.

The doctor pulled out a hand-held device.

"This is the detector," said Knight. "This is what law enforcement will be given to find the devices."

To prove that his technology was working, he held his arm out while the doctor turned on the machine. It immediately started beeping. Knight and the doctor both smiled.

"This is just the first part of the program," he noted. "The chips are programmable, even after they are injected."

Knight then held up another device and explained the procedure for coding the chip. A technician was on hand for the day. Once a chip was implanted, its number was recorded into the device. The technician then simply typed in information about the child. When a child is reported missing, the information will be in a database, and law enforcement will then know for which number to look.

"Please note that the device just beeped," noted Knight, who then took the device from the tech. "And here is my name on the screen."

His entourage applauded.

Knight held the cotton ball against his arm, walked over to the window, then waived to the crowd.

The group quickly made its way to the waiting limo. Knight's phone started to ring as he put his mask back on. The message was from his New York City friend.

"I can't believe you went through with that," it said.

"I didn't. It was sugar water," was Absalom's reply. "The whole thing was faked. They do work, but I'm in the inner circle. We don't track ourselves."

He looked up and noticed that his bodyguard was staring. Absalom realized he made the mistake of wearing his mask in front of someone who had not seen him before. Once he got into his gated home, he pulled out a gun and killed the guard as they sat in the back of the vehicle.

Knight had removed the mask before another guard opened the door.

"Put him with the others," said Knight on the way to speak with his female captains.

"Now on to phase three," he said as the three sat down to an early dinner. "But that won't happen until tomorrow."

Chapter 15

"Busy week I see," said Green as she approached Lamplighter at the Wal-Mart garden center.

"Yeah, get that a lot," replied Lamplighter as he looked up from behind a grill.

"Doesn't surprise me," she replied. "With the week you've had I'm glad that you are still with our committee."

Lamplighter looked around the crowded garden center before answering.

"I made a commitment to help," he replied. "Plus, I had a lot of fun last year so I want to do it again."

Green held a pot filled with three colors of pansies. Then picked out some petals that had fallen from one of the blooms.

"Well," said Green, "if I didn't say it yet, I want to say that the committee appreciates all of your hard work."

Reminded that he still had a grill to build, Lamplighter reached down to pick up the not-yet-attached top to the grill he was about to finish.

"How did you say it?" he asked. "With many hands there is a lighter load."

"Something like that," laughed Green. "But I expected another patriotic quote from you."

"OK, umm," said Lamplighter as he placed the cover into its notches. "How about Thomas Paine? 'Our citizenship in the United States is our national character. Our citizenship in any particular state is only our local distinction. By the latter, we are known at home, by the former to the world. Our great title is Americans.'"

"Where do you get all these from?" she asked.

"I kept one of my college textbooks," noted Lamplighter.

"On that note, I am going to check out," said Green. "See you Saturday."

Lamplighter responded in kind, then went right back to his grill. He had placed the project along the center of the showroom's walls. From that vantage point, Lamplighter could build the grill while still watching for long lines at the register. He filled in on several occasions already during the first two hours of the day's shift.

With July 4 coming up on a weekend and just three shifts away, Wal-Mart management mandated that garden center employees push the grills, grill accessories and lawn furniture that customers could use for their entertaining. One of those customers was the same man who had been tailing him all week.

Lamplighter had a variety of grills to construct. He started the day with a dictionary sized model that instantly sold to a young woman with two children. He started this build which was in the middle of the available sizes, 45 minutes ago and finished it just before his break.

"Got time for a chess game?" asked Matt, a common break-room opponent.

"Nope, just a 15," replied Lamplighter as poured himself a cup of coffee and sat next to his friend.

The television was set on the 24-hour news channel.

"You have to be kidding me," said Lamplighter as the station cut to Knight's pre-injection press conference. "Don't people know who this guy is?"

He explained to Matt about Knight's involvement in the secret society.

"He's got to be up to something," Lamplighter continued.

He made mental notes of the conference while also trying to listen to his co-workers at other tables. The majority of them approved of the RFID chips.

"Wow," Lamplighter said as he watched Knight walk into the doctor's office. "People are actually buying this?"

He watched as Knight got his shot.

"I wouldn't be surprised to find out if that were fake, too," said Lamplighter before checking the clock and heading back to work.

He just shook his head as he walked toward the garden center. Lamplighter helped customers find a hammer, bird feeder, cat food and oil for a lawn mower.

One of his favorite tricks is to use his cane to reach things for customers. It came in handy for the cat food as Wal-Mart's last can of the elderly woman's favorite variety was out of both of their reach. His method was to grab the cane near the bottom and corral the can with the handle. It was successful, much to the appreciation of the woman.

'That comes in handy I see," said the customer.

Lamplighter chuckled.

"Something that I got for my leg comes in handy," he said with a smile.

The woman just stared at him.

"That was a lame joke, but I give you credit that you tried," she replied, then turn and walked away.

"Ha! Lame joke," he thought while tapping the rubber bottom of his cane against his bad ankle. "I'll have to use that pun on somebody else."

He noticed the long lines as soon as he took the right-hand turn into the outdoor section and went right for the registers.

Lamplighter spent the next two hours checking out people's orders before heading back for lunch.

Out came his cell phone as soon as he got into the break room.

"I saw this guy get an RFID chip can I please write a story about it?" was the message he sent to the editor of the health magazine.

The second was for Gloria.

"Lunch time."

Lamplighter, who hadn't eaten in seven hours, wolfed down his turkey sandwich and apple lunch before gathering all of the papers in the room. He studied one article that basically rehashed Tuesday's press conference. It disturbed him that the Knight did not take any questions but referred all reporters to a press release.

His phone buzzed again as soon as Lamplighter finished the story.

"I just sent you an email," replied the editor. "We got a press release from him. I will send this to you. Don't forget to interview people against the RFID."

"Oh, I will," thought Lamplighter before responding.

He took a sip of coffee then started the reply.

"Thank you for the assignment. I look forward to completing it," he said.

Lamplighter reread the article, then watched the news for a story on Knight and what his plan might be. The reporter summed up the event and showed only about 30 seconds of video. Lamplighter observed more coworkers nod in response.

He took another drink from his coffee cup.

"Looks like I have my work cut out for me," he thought.

Chapter 16

Gloria Lamplighter is a hard worker. She applied to be a cashier at Dollar General two years ago, but due to her extensive experience in retail, Gloria was instantly hired for the assistant manager job. Once she passed all of her training tests, she was shipped around to help at several stores in the Canandaigua area.

The manager who hired her was promoted to district manager just three weeks ago. Gloria was then elevated to acting assistant manager. Her first task was to get the store ready for its annual inspection, which would be conducted by the same manager who hired her.

"I've got to get this right," she said as she left for work on Wednesday morning.

Gloria's plan was to work as many hours as she could to get her store cleaned while letting her two assistant managers run it. She arrived 45 minutes before Nathan, the assistant she scheduled to work the morning shift.

The inspection was set for Monday. It was a date set at random and intended for the store's original manager.

"I was thrust into this, but it's a chance to prove myself," she thought as she started cleaning.

Gloria started by organizing the back office and finished just as Nathan checked in. Her next task was to get the stockroom ready for the arrival of the weekly truck, which was always scheduled for Friday.

She took a 15-minute break at 11 a.m., then took over the front register to relieve Nathan.

"Good job," he said upon his return.

"Welcome," responded Gloria. "And thank you for your help."

Gloria finished off the stockroom, then cleaned the bathroom. It was now 2 p.m. and time to work up front so Nathan could take his lunch. She spent time working on the store's product displays between customers. A cashier arrived just as Nathan's lunch was over.

"OK," said Gloria. "Time for me to go home for a bit."

She got to the townhouse in time to watch a news report about the missing children.

"And now my husband is caught up in that, too," she thought has she rubbed the cat, which had leaped onto her lap.

Gloria grabbed a quick lunch of a ham sandwich and Mountain Dew before taking a short nap. She arrived back at the store at 4:30 p.m., one hour after her other assistant manager, Laurel Smith, had taken over for the night.

"Whew," said Gloria as she walked past the register. "I needed that."

She dropped off her purse in the break room and immediately set back up front to give Smith her break. After that, the two worked tirelessly to clean the entire store for the night. In between customers, the two and the cashier made sure that the floor was swept clean and every product was put in its proper place.

"Well, that looks great." said Smith as they headed back to the office around 8:15 p.m. to count the day's till.

Gloria noted that it was one of the highest totals she had seen in three months.

"Fourth of July," noted Gloria. "People are getting ready for the holiday."

Smith waited for her sister to pick her up by sitting on a short brick wall just outside the store for her ride home. As per company policy, the ranking person on the shift, Gloria, had to be the last person to leave the property. After finishing her in-store duties, she took a seat next to her coworker.

"I would do this anyway," said Gloria.

Gloria took a drink of soda.

"Good idea," said Smith, who then took a sip from her own beverage. "I wonder where my sister is, but then again, she is always late."

The two chatted about their personals lives while waiting.

"Sorry about the wait," said Smith before sending her sister a text message to ask her why she was late.

Ten minutes later, a man who appeared drunk banged on the door.

"Sorry we are closed," said Gloria.

The man ignored her and cupped his hands together to peek through the door into the now dark building. He then banged harder on the door.

"We are closed for the evening," said Gloria. "Maybe IGA up the block can help you."

The man who was the same height as both women approached them with closed fists.

"Open this door or I will make you open this door," he shouted with a slur.

"Sorry, but I can't do that," said a frazzled Gloria, who tried to sound calm. "We have already closed the store."

Gloria and Laurel dashed into the Lamplighters' car and locked the doors, but the man followed and banged on the driver's side window. Gloria called 9-1-1 and talked loudly enough so that the man could hear what she was saying, but the man still did not stop shouting.

"Dammit," he yelled. "Open the store."

A small boy, dressed in only a T-shirt and a diaper, walked over, sat against the wall, and started to cry for his daddy. Unmoved by the sight of the child, the attacker continued banging on the front window. Smith dug into Gloria's purse to find a canister of pepper spray.

Gloria rolled down her window just enough to aim her weapon. Their attacker returned to her side of the car. She pressed the trigger.

"What the hell did you do that for?" shouted the man as he fell to the ground.

He backed off just as a police car arrived, then another. The parking lot became as crowded as a big-city rush hour when Smith's sister arrived. An ambulance was called to help take care of the attacker, who had fallen and hit his head.

Smith's sister had corralled the crying child and asked who he was. This prompted one of the police officers to call an agent from child protective services. That last car to arrive contained Detective Ryne and Lamplighter.

The normally even-keeled Gloria ran into her husband's arms and finally started crying.

"How did you get here?" she asked after gaining her composure.

"Thank Detective Ryne for that," replied Don.

The crowd migrated three blocks east to the Canandaigua Police Department headquarters, where Gloria and Smith gave their statements. It was determined that the child was on the missing lists but was actually reported missing with a note of a possible family abduction. Gloria's attacker was the biological father but lost custody due to an alcohol problem.

"It looks like this time you solved a case," Lamplighter said to his wife.

He took his turn at the wheel to let Gloria rest. She just nodded in response with a small tear making its way down her cheek.

The Lamplighters got food from McDonald's before heading home. Because of the new RFID assignment, Lamplighter wanted to get some writing done but decided that it would be more important to comfort his wife. The two ate while watching a romantic comedy.

The verses for the family's night Bible study were Romans chapter 14 and 15. The verses explained how to teach the message of Christ to others.

Gloria took comfort in chapter 14, verse 19: "Therefore let us pursue the things that make for peace and the things by which we may edify another."

"I hope what we did saved that child tonight," she said. "And that what you do helps other children."

The Lamplighters went to bed together around 1:30 a.m.

"I came home for a break today and watched the news," noted Gloria. "It gave a report on the missing children."

She rolled over to face her husband.

"I thought 'and my husband is in the middle of it,'" continued Gloria. "Now I'm caught up in this, too."

Chapter 17

Gloria's God-given resolve would not let her deviate from her plan to whip her store into shape. She left Thursday morning to get to her work at 8 a.m. The plan gave her husband a unique opportunity. Normally when his wife took the early shift, he would have to take the bus to Wal-Mart. Today, Gloria planned to come home for a rest and take her husband to his work.

Lamplighter didn't get up until 10:30 a.m.

He first did his morning Bible study. His quest had reached Isaiah Chapters 35-39. Lamplighter learned of Hezakiah's prayer and God's response. He drew strength from Chapter 35, verse 4: "Say to those who have an anxious heart,

"Be strong; fear not!

Behold, your God

will come with vengeance,

with the recompense of God.

He will come and save you."

Lamplighter has a particular reason to skip breakfast and head straight to his writing. He had two priorities - send away the stories on the garden and Clifton Springs doctor and get a good start on the child abduction and RFID articles. With no time off until the Sunday deadlines, Lamplighter had to take every second of free time to finish his journalistic obligations.

He long ago figured out that he needed to give his contacts as much time as possible to return phone calls. Lamplighter cleared his throat and warmed up voice by reciting one of his many favorite patriotic quotes - a verse from the American Soldier's Hymn.

"Tis God that girds our armor on and all our just designs fulfills; through Him our feet can swiftly run and numbly climb the steepest hills."

He then searched through his business card collection for Detective Ryne to gather any information on the abductions. Lamplighter wasn't sure if he could get a hold of him and was right, as he ended up leaving a message. He continued the work on the story by trying to reach Sheriff Cornell, again being forced to leave a message.

After that, Lamplighter attempted to get interviews for the RFID story. He first called the bank owned by Ken Knight. Knight's secretary was instructed not to let reporters through, telling each one to refer to the press releases. Lamplighter was frustrated by the stonewalling and eventually just left a message. He was equally rejected in his attempt to reach Dr. Black, getting the same response - read the press release. Lamplighter again left a message.

"Well, that went nowhere," he thought as he stood up and stretched.

Lamplighter finally switched on his computer. It was the first time he saw the email from the health magazine editor. As promised, there was a second email with the press release from Knight. Lamplighter printed it out.

There was also a message from the Victor News editor, requesting an update on his stories. Lamplighter responded before getting to his proofreading work.

He developed a four-step process for editing his articles. Lamplighter first read through the story for a general review. Next was to run it through his computer's spell check. After that, Lamplighter did a fact check. Finally, he read the article aloud.

His first target was the garden story. Lamplighter took 35 minutes to put it through his wringer. He then attached the photos and sent them off in a reply to the Victor News editor's earlier email.

Lamplighter took a break to watch the midday news on one of the Rochester network affiliates. One of the bigger stories was last night's recovery of one of the missing children. The story gave a quick reference to the Lamplighters being involved and what led to the recovery of the boy. It followed that by a rehashing on Knight's antics at Dr. Black's clinic. Just like with him, the TV reporters were not able to get any more interview time with either of them.

"Frustrating for media, but I have to give him credit for the discipline to follow the script," thought Lamplighter. "But what is the end game of the script?"

He then applied the steps to the doctor story. This was a longer story and took him 50 minutes to complete the process. Lamplighter added three pictures of the physician - a mug shot, a portrait of him in his lab and an action shot of him taking care of a patient.

"I'm still surprised I got permission for that," he said.

Lamplighter went back downstairs to preheat the oven and feed the cat. Back in his office, he watched clips of both of Knight's press conferences and gave his printer a workout with research on RFID. He put a pizza in the oven before returning to print out some statistics on missing children.

According to a study, he found online, Federal Bureau of Investigation statistics show that a child is abducted in the United States every 40 seconds.

"That is alarming," he thought.

The FBI divides child-kidnapping cases into those abducted by family members, those abducted by acquaintances and those who are taken by strangers.

"That case I am working on falls into the last group," he thought.

He found further information - strangers are more likely to abduct females over males and the study shows that these are liable to happen outdoors. Lamplighter was shocked to find out that approximately 20 percent of non-family abductions are not found alive and of those, 74 percent are murdered within the first three hours.

"I guess I have to work faster on these," he said aloud with a sigh.

Lamplighter made a special note that the study claims that stranger abductees are likely to be taken off the street or lured into a vehicle.

The alarming stats inspired him to work on his Wing Chun and cane fighting. After going through his practice routines, he watered the plants.

Lamplighter then showered and got dressed in his Wal-Mart uniform as Gloria came home from the first half of her shift at Dollar General. They kissed right before he surprised her with the pizza - her lunch and his breakfast. After the meal, they headed out.

"That's a cute poodle," said Gloria as they stopped to wait for a man walking his dog to cross the sidewalk over the exit to the complex.

"He doesn't look anything like the description the cops gave us," replied Lamplighter, who then shrugged his shoulders. "About the same height, though."

"And that is a cute dog," she added.

Gloria dropped Lamplighter off at the Garden Center, but not before getting another earful of Gregg Matzek's Independence Day statements. It was a statement by John Adams.

"The Revolution was affected before the war commenced. The Revolution was in the minds and hearts of the people ... This radical change in the principles, opinions, sentiments and affections of the people was the real American Revolution."

Still unknown to Lamplighter, the same made had followed them all the way.

Chapter 18

"How is phase three going?" asked the marketing executive from New York City.

"My security company is working on it now," replied Knight while eating lunch from his office high above the downtown Rochester skyline. "Soon every parent in this city will want the RFID chips."

The executive looked out the window of his office. His window design allowed him to have a panoramic view of the Big Apple. The conversation started with him looking over Brooklyn.

"Then we will take this to my city," replied the marketing executive.

Knight took a bite and pondered that statement. He liked it when a well-thought-out plan comes to fruition.

"Phase two worked great," said Knight after chasing down his meal with a gulp of orange soda. "Did you see that TV news clip?"

"Of course I watched," replied the executive. "Good job."

Knight leaned back in his chair.

"That security team was owned by one of my captains," noted Knight. "We estimated that there would be 300 people that showed up, we counted 641."

"Twice as many as we expected," replied the executive, who then switched windows to look over the Statue of Liberty. "Of course you ordered less than that number."

"Yes we made sure of that," said Knight. "Planned scarcity; the lack of availability of a product will make you want it more, just like we learned at the solstice gathering."

Knight's secretary knocked on the door.

"Phone call from Don Lamplighter," she said.

"What does he want?" asked Knight.

"He wants to talk about the RFID," replied the secretary.

"I heard that," said the executive. "Stay to the script."

"Tell him that I am unavailable," ordered Knight. "Get his information and send him the press release."

The secretary got to the door before Knight again got her attention.

"Oh and please leave me alone until I say so," he said.

The secretary nodded and left the room.

"Is there a problem?" asked the executive.

"Just Don Lamplighter trying to reach me about the RFID," said Knight. "I am going to put you on hold for a moment."

Knight walked around his office to make sure that every curtain covering an outside office window was closed. He then pulled the shades to prevent him from been seen by any of his bank employees. Knight then got back into his chair and pulled his Absalom mask from his briefcase. The lights were turned off by remote control, leaving the room completely dark.

Knight put on the mask before resuming his conversation.

"That's better," said Knight as he resumed the conversation. "I felt like wearing my disguise."

"Either way," replied the executive. "Why don't you just kill that guy?"

"Believe me, I would like too," added Knight. "But it is not that simple."

Knight followed up by recalling how Lamplighter had rescued the baby and saved the girls from the pedophile ring on Monday.

"So he is kind of a celebrity around here," he noted. "If we kill him the investigation will be bigger than anything we want right now."

The executive leaned back in his chair and started rolling metal stress balls in his hand.

"Good point," he said. "As the public relations officer for this state, I advise you not to do that right now. Especially over this RFID thing."

Knight tapped his fingers on his desk.

"I am handling reporters for this by just sticking to the script," he said. 'There are two ways that this can go bad for us."

Knight paused to take a sip of orange soda.

"One: enough of those crazy conspiracy junkies speak out," he notes. "We got that countered with our propaganda and red herring arguments."

"You have to think the Earth is flat is you believe that," interrupted the executive. "We have been using that one for years."

"Exactly," said Knight. "The other is if he finds out that the company that produces the chips is owned by our organization. We have so many shell companies that Lamplighter will not find that out."

The executive leaned forward in his chair.

"You realize that you eventually might have to kill him," he said.

"Oh I know," replied Knight. "Once, or even if, he figures out our organization, he will be dealt with."

Knight grabbed a gun out of his desk drawer and pretended to fire a shot.

"But until then he will be of use to us," he said. "We can feed him stories that make us look good."

"True," added the executive. "Just like we do to the rest of the journalists, or at least most of them."

Knight put the gun down.

"The other thing is this pedophile ring that is operating around here," he said. "If Lamplighter helps take that apart and it is identified with other people, it puts less heat on us."

Knight sat on his desk.

"Plus these people will have to go through all of the legal proceedings," he notes. "Each time their face is in the news it will terrify people and send more of them to the RFID chips."

"Another win for us," said the executive.

Knight's phone beeped indicating that he received another call. He sat back into his chair.

"I am going to have to put you on hold again," he said after recognizing the number as that of Vic, his security guru.

"Phase three is planned and ready to go," said Vic. "We have picked out the mark and have everything in place."

Knight leaned back in his chair.

"Well, then commence the operation," he said with a smile.

Knight switched the line back to the executive.

"Well, it looks like we have phase three starting," he noted. "I will talk to you later, my friend."

The executive responded with equal salutations.

"Oh and one more thing," said Knight. "I beat Don Lamplighter in chess."

Knight made one more call before removing his mask and setting his office back for business - this one was to one of his friends in New York.

"Please make sure that your friend does not interrupt me again," he said.

Chapter 19

Lamplighter gave his wife a kiss in front of the center group of the three Wal-Mart super center entrances. All employees must use this entrance when both starting and leaving their shift. Gloria likes it because it has a large section for loading merchandise. She uses this area to turn around and head back out of the parking lot. Don likes it because it has the biggest doors, which allow him more space to get through, given the wide berth he requires while using his cane.

Mike, the greeter, likes it because it allows him to view a majority of the parking lot.

"That guy fell down while holding his chest," he said to Lamplighter.

Lamplighter turned around to see a man lying on the concrete right in the way of the row of cars.

"Just clutching his chest you say?" he asked.

"Yes," replied Mike. "He held his chest and just fell down."

Lamplighter rapidly limped across the busy traffic in front of the store to get to the victim. There was a young woman with him.

"I already called 9-1-1," said the woman, who was holding her baby.

"Thank you," responded Lamplighter. "Are you related or do you otherwise know him?"

"No, just a bystander," she said.

Lamplighter was trained in both first aid and CPR when he was in Boys Scouts. He has since updated that through several courses. He checked for a pulse on both his wrist and neck. Finding none, he then checked for breathing. He got negative results.

"Did you see him take any medication," Lamplighter asked the bystander

"No," was the simple reply.

"OK," continued Lamplighter. "Did anyone or anything hit him?"

"Not that I saw," said the witness. "He just grabbed his chest, started falling, reached out to that parked car, slid off and hit the ground,"

Lamplighter directed a passing cart pusher to call for management before asking a final question.

"Did he hit his head," he said while again checking for a pulse.

"He landed on his side," she said.

Lamplighter remembered a story he had done regarding new guidelines for CPR. According to the rules, if you know when the person fell, you only have to perform what is called hands-only CPR, which is 100 chest compressions per minutes without rescue breathing. This was done because organizations felt that people had an increasing fear of performing mouth-to-mouth resuscitation due to the chance of catching a communicable disease.

Lamplighter gave one more check for a pulse before starting chest compressions.

"One and two and three and four and five," he said aloud as a crowd gathered.

The group of bystanders included two Wal-Mart employees who were leaving for the day, a member of the town of Hopewell Fire Department, Norton from the city committee and about 10 people that Lamplighter did not know.

"I'll take a turn now," said the fireman as Lamplighter took the other a side of the victim to check for a pulse.

"I think I've got something," he said while examining the patient's wrist.

The crowd parted to allow for an ambulance to arrive. Store management got to the scene while the rescue personnel was getting the man, who was both breathing and had a pulse, into the ambulance.

"You realize I need a report on this," said the manager as she checked her watch. "You are also late for your shift. You better go check in."

Norton followed Lamplighter into the store.

"You know, you have had a pretty rough couple of weeks," said Norton. "Why don't you come over for a party tomorrow night? I'm inviting everyone on the committee to join me."

"I appreciate the invitation," responded Lamplighter. "But I must politely decline since I work tomorrow night as well."

Norton paused as the two continued to walk to the back of the store.

"OK, well if you can make it, why don't you and your wife come out on my boat with me for the fireworks?" he asked.

'That is something we would both like to do," responded Lamplighter. "I have a volunteer shift at the park that night and Gloria has to work, but I will see what we can do."

Lamplighter checked in and had a typically mixed, but busy first two hours of his shift. His time was spent between building grills, working on the register and helping customers find items in the store. He counted six boxes that he carried out to cars.

"Quite the parade of people coming through here," said Regis. "Not as long as the one you have to direct Saturday, though."

"But I can be in this one," replied Lamplighter in an excited tone.

Another favorite cane trick of his was to use it as a musical instrument. The opening inside the handle was about the same size as that of a trumpet mouthpiece. Lamplighter presses the cane to his lips and makes the same buzz that he uses when he plays in the band. The cane has no mechanism to change notes, so he just plays the same one eight times and laughs.

Regis just shook his head.

"Go and take your break," said the department manager. "And don't forget to give your report."

"Pretty straight-forward story," he thought as he headed to the management office to give his account of the earlier medical emergency.

Lamplighter followed that by taking his 15-minute break. He read two newspaper articles about last night's incident with Gloria.

"Well, they got the facts right," he said.

One of the stories included a graphic of all of the children that went missing during the past couple of weeks. He had already made one for himself but cut this one out any way.

Lamplighter put the information in his wallet, finished his coffee and headed out for the second two hours of his shift. It was similar to the first quarter - busy enough to make the time go fast, but not busy enough to be stressful.

Lamplighter considered the case during his brief moments of peace.

"There has got to be a connection here," he thought.

Chapter 20

Garfield rehearsed the plan with his mark again.

"You showed up at the right time, 6:30 p.m. just like when we contacted you," he said as he pulled up to the young lady. "Now scream and pretend like you are trying to get away."

The woman performed her assigned acting job as Garfield pulled her child into the junker they stole for the event.

"Good job," he said. "Your $55,000 will be sent to you shortly."

Garfield quickly blindfolded the child before he drove off in a northerly direction on Dewey Avenue on the western side of Rochester.

The young lady was contacted four hours earlier by an agent of Garfield. She was selected from a list of people who had their children implanted with the RFID chip. The situation fit all of the qualifications needed - a young woman, single with only one kid. Knight's computer research indicated that she worked at a lower-paying job and would probably be easily paid off as long as she was promised that her eight-year-old boy would be safe the whole time. He was correct.

"Wow, I could use this money," she thought as she watched the car drive away. "All I have to do is keep my mouth shut."

She acted like she was in shock, then started screaming again two minutes later. Just like she was supposed to do. A crowd of her neighbors gathered, including her mother, who called 9-1-1.

"I tried to save my son but he was too strong," she cried. "I tried."

Her mother gave her a hug, saying nothing, but rubbing her daughter's back. The young woman kept crying

"You got the RFID tag right?" asked one neighbor. "We will see if Knight and his device work."

That was the entire point of the exercise.

Garfield kept driving until he hit Lake Street. He took a quick right until he reached an abandoned two-story building. He parked in an area hidden from view and took the child out. So to not attract attention, he took the child and walked at a normal pace to a door. Once there, he removed the blindfold and headed upstairs.

"OK, I got him here," Garfield said into a burner phone as he set the kid down into the center of a vacant apartment.

"Understood," replied Vic through a second cheap cell phone. "Follow the next steps and meet me at the spot we picked."

"I'm on it already," he said.

Vic listened to his portable emergency scanner. Police were acting just as planned. First he heard one car arrive next to the young woman and her mother, then he heard a second and a third.

"I don't know cars that well," said the young woman. "It was four doors, silver and kind of old looking."

A fourth police car arrived, followed by an ambulance.

"You better hurry up," Vic said in a second call to Garfield. "The cops are getting to the abduction scene faster than we thought."

Garfield complied by quickly showing the child around the room. He had previously set up a small TV and put in some kid's movie to keep him occupied until the chip did its job. Also left in the apartment was a pile of food and some juice. Garfield then made sure that the toilet worked before leaving.

"Don't cry, kid," he said. "Your mommy will find you soon."

As he instructed, he removed the battery from his phone and drove to the Genesee River, where he tossed the phone into the water.

Vic's emergency scanner was buzzing as the police said that bystanders had given a better description of the vehicle. The young woman also gave intentionally vague notes on Garfield to further aid in his escape.

"This is cutting it way too close," thought Vic.

Garfield drove on some lesser-used streets and dropped the junker in front of a lot that used to be a video store, but had gone out of business years ago. He then walked two blocks west, one block north and another three blocks west before finding Vic.

"Good job," Vic said to his favorite goon has he headed back across the river to Knight's house. "Now all we have to do is sit and wait until the chip brings the cops to the kid."

Knight met the pair in the drawing room.

"One more question," said Vic as he put his arm around Garfield. "Did you take care of your messenger like we said?"

"Yeah," he replied. "In the trunk of that car."

"Good go bring her to the fire pit," Vic ordered.

Garfield carried the dead body. He slid her into the pit and turned around to smile at Vic, who promptly stabbed him through the heart and shoved him into the pit as well.

Knight approached the pit to find the bodies of both Garfield and his messenger ready for cremation,

"That just leaves three people that know the truth about this," Knight he said as he turned up the heat in the pit and took a sip from a bottle of orange soda. "Let's go talk about something else," he gathered his captains for another meeting.

"In front of you is a report on Don Lamplighter," he said.

Each of his captains opened the manila folder.

"Vic had one of his operatives follow him," he said. "I also hacked his computer and tracked his cell phone."

Absalom folded his collection of information and tapped it on the table.

"I admit that he does write some interesting stories," he said. "But other than that, he is so clean cut that he might bore me to death before I get a chance to kill him."

His captains laughed.

"I'm thinking about calling off my mini task force on him," he said. "Any suggestions?"

"I will keep an ear out for him," said Vic. "But other than that, I don't think anything else is necessary."

"Agreed," added Madame Stephanie. "I will have my ladies report back to me if they hear anything, then take care of him should the need arise."

"That will deprive me of the satisfaction of killing somebody," said Absalom as he turned to Vic. "Do you have that homeless guy ready?"

Vic nodded.

'Are you sure you want to do this?" he asked.

"Of course," replied Absalom. "For our global takeover plan to succeed about two billion people worldwide have to die consider this getting used to it.

Vic nodded again

"OK," said Absalom with a sigh.. "Let's take him to the firing range, then come back and watch TV."

Chapter 21

Lamplighter had a bad taste in his mouth, and it wasn't from the free coffee from the break room.

"They don't want to tell me what these kids all have in common," he thought. "But it is more frustrating to me that I can't figure this out."

Lamplighter had already finished his lunch of a turkey sandwich, baby carrots, and apple. He took his competitor's list of missing children out of his wallet and crossed off all of those that were suspected taken by relatives.

'That narrows it down," he thought as he beamed with pride over his wife's bravery.

Lamplighter held the document at arm's length, then set it back on the table.

"There. I think I got them all, but I still don't get it," he thought.

Lamplighter started playing with the list. He looked at it upside down. He looked at it sideways and finally spun it around on the table under his finger.

"I don't think you can read it that way," jested Mike the greeter as he took the seat to Lamplighter's right.

"I can't figure it out no matter how I look at it," replied Lamplighter. "I have it shaved down to those that are suspected to have been abducted by a stranger."

He stopped spinning the list and passed it over to his coworker.

"But look," said Lamplighter. "The kids are different, the methods are different and the places where the bodies were found have nothing in common."

"I see your point," said Mike as he passed it back to Lamplighter.

"But here is the thing," added Lamplighter. "When we are at the park in Victor, the sheriff knew right away that it was part of the same case. Why?"

Lamplighter and Mike went quiet to listen to the start of the 6:30 news. The broadcast was led off by yet another candidate joining the 2016 race for the presidency. This time it was a Republican senator from Alaska. That made it four candidates from each party. Also in line for the GOP were a former Army general from New York, the governor of Arizona and a businessman from Delaware. Contesting the race for the Democratic nomination were the ambassador to France, two senators - one each from Missouri and Maryland - and the former governor of California. The analyst expected even more people to throw their hat in the ring.

"As usual, a pretty bad crowd to choose from," said Mike. "I don't want to vote for any of them."

"I don't know for whom I will vote," added Lamplighter. "I will wait to see who gets third-party nominations."

They both struggled to hear the news over the rest of the conversations in the break room. Lamplighter was disappointed that there was nothing about the missing children.

"You know," said Lamplighter. "I am doing a story on this, so I have to find out."

He pulled out his cell phone and sent a text to the sheriff.

"I'm going to work on the story tonight. Do you have any updates from Victor?"

Lamplighter refilled his coffee cup as he waited for his response.

"A second cup already?" asked Mike.

"Yeah," responded Lamplighter with a sigh. "I have two more stories to finish tonight."

He started spinning his phone when it started to vibrate.

"I don't have time now," replied the sheriff. "I can send you the press release."

'That will do for now," typed Lamplighter. "But we do have to meet."

Further texting led to a meeting Friday during Lamplighter's lunch break.

He leaned back in his chair and let out a yawn.

"At least I got a meeting with him," he said.

Lamplighter texted a love note to Gloria before being challenged to a chess match by a male coworker to whom he was not yet introduced. The game lasted right up until the time Lamplighter had to get back to his shift. He used a quick back-rank mate to end the contest with a victory just in time to get back to work.

"Thank you for the game," said Lamplighter during a gentlemanly post-game handshake.

The next two hours of the shift were a continuance of the first four, with his time being divided between building grills and working the register.

An army veteran went through the line just as he was about to close down.

"Interesting shirt," said Lamplighter.

The veteran recited its wording verbatim.

"Give me liberty or give me death," said the veteran. "My favorite."

"I have to memorize that one," replied Lamplighter.

"Well, happy fourth of July," said the veteran as he left the store.

Lamplighter closed up the register before heading back for his break. He nearly spits out his coffee.

"Police credit the RFID chip and the detector donated by Ken Knight with finding the child," said the reporter.

Lamplighter, along with the other three workers in the room, sat quietly listening to the story. First to interview was the Rochester police chief.

"I thank Ken Knight and his chips for saving his child," he said. "He was one of the fortunate children in the area who received a free chip from Knight."

The police chief further explained that several of his officers were driven through the city using detectors that were tuned to the frequency of the chip. Once the chip was found, they sent in a SWAT unit into the building and saved the child, who was unharmed.

"We didn't find the perpetrator, but the area police departments are putting in our best efforts on the case."

He was followed by the young woman, who was holding her son through the entire conversation.

"How convenient," noted Lamplighter.

"Are you saying that he set this up?" asked Mike.

"I wouldn't be surprised if we find out that he did," replied Lamplighter. "Make people want to come to him to get the chip instead of forcing us to get one."

One of the bystanders spoke next, followed by the officer that actually found the child.

"I can see what you mean," said Mike.

"Knight has promised a press conference for 10 a.m. tomorrow," closed the news anchor.

"I have to watch that," thought Lamplighter.

He exchanged more love notes with his wife before returning to the garden center. Given the hot weather, he spent the remaining hour and a half watering the plants in all three of the outdoor sections. The quiet allowed Lamplighter to contemplate the case and how he was going to write his story.

"Nope," he thought. "Still can't figure it out."

Gloria picked him up at 11 p.m. They discussed their nights at work before getting home. Gloria watched as her husband removed the lanyard that holds his Wal-Mart employee tag. It featured the Batman symbol and often served as a conversation started with his customers.

"That reminds me," said Gloria. "I saw Captain Morgan in my store earlier. He bought a whole bunch of stickers with heroes on them."

"The church does host the city's after-school program," added Lamplighter, who looked down at his lanyard with Batman logos on it. "Maybe it's for them. I'm kind of jealous, actually."

They shared some reheated fast-food burgers for dinner.

Gloria's Bible study pick started on Luke chapter 9. The five-chapter grouping included both the story of the Good Samaritan and the Lord's Prayer. The Lamplighters discussed the meaning of Chapter 10, verse 27 "So he answered and said, 'You shall love the Lord with all your heart, with all your soul, with all your strength and with all your mind and your neighbor as yourself.'"

The both agreed that their actions reflected this instruction.

"OK," said Lamplighter as he kissed his wife. "Time to get to work."

He received the sheriff's press release via an email. He typed a basic story but left gaps that he expected to fill after their planned interview.

Next, the typed a longer story on the RFID chips using the written statements provided by both Knight and Dr. Black.

"That's not good enough," he thought

Lamplighter then did a search for groups that opposed the devices. One of them included the Jeff McLowery family from Farmington, the township between Victor and Canandaigua. He quickly sent off an email requesting an interview. He made a note to call them back after watching Knight's press conference, which by now was only six hours away.

Lamplighter did his nightly random Bible study.

He set his alarm and crawled into bed with Gloria. It was another hour before he could finally get to sleep.

"I still can't figure it out," he thought.

Chapter 22

Lamplighter dreaded getting less than six hours of sleep. What made Friday morning worse is that he had to get up early to watch more of his archenemy's lies.

"Hrgumph," he mumbled as he stretched out to turn off his alarm clock. "Already."

Lamplighter got up at 9:45 a.m., fifteen minutes before the press conference, but just five hours after he finally drifted to sleep. He stretched as he got out of bed, changed from his pajamas into a polo shirt and shorts and headed downstairs. After feeding the cat, he set up his vintage VCR to record the event.

"Unfortunately," Lamplighter grumbled. "I can't miss this."

He barely kept himself awake for the slim five-minute wait time from when the TV news anchor announced the start of the media event until Knight made his appearance. Lamplighter pressed on his video recorder as soon at Knight started to speak.

'Thank you all for coming," said Knight. "This shows that Rochester actually does care about its children."

"Again that line," thought Lamplighter. "People still fall for that."

He watched the show through half-closed eyes as Knight recalled the events of the night before.

"I would like to thank the efforts of the task force," continued Knight as he pointed out the members of the law enforcement community that gathered behind him. "The speed at which the missing boy was recovered was due to their diligence and hard work."

Members of the audience clapped as the camera panned past every member of the task force. Lamplighter recognized both Sheriff Cornell and Detective Ryne.

"Yeesh," he thought. "And I thought I didn't get any sleep."

Knight then repeated some statistics about crime in the Rochester area, New York State and the nation. He moved his arm to again draw attention to the members of the law enforcement community.

"These brave servants behind me have shown that things are only going to get better," he said. "Our communities are going to be safer for our children because of them."

A second camera provided a view of the entire crowd as it erupted into yet another round of applause. Lamplighter noticed that protestors were conspicuous by their absence.

The news pointed out the mother of the rescued child.

"Actually smart," he thought. "With the mother there, they even look more like heroes."

Immediately after that Knight introduced the young woman and her child.

"This young woman and her son showed courage in the face of danger by trying to fight off their attacker and strength of spirit by keeping her faith while the community searched for her missing child," Knight said, patting the young boy on top of the head.

"Absolutely shameless self-promotion," thought Lamplighter. "Then again, this guy is pure evil so I should have expected that."

"This young family, as well as several other members of the Rochester area, also showed wisdom in accepting my offer of free RFID chips," added Knight. "Had they not of done that, we might still be looking for him."

Lamplighter put his head into his hands.

"So I see the game here," Lamplighter said aloud. "Take advantage of the situation to further agenda, just like Gregg Matzek explains. I have to get going on that story."

Knight then noted that he had ordered 1,000 more chips and that they would be administered by Dr. Black. They would notify the media of their arrival and when the clinic will be open for the procedure.

"Just like I said in the break room," he said to the family cat. "Trick us into running to him for help."

Knight then sneaked back into his limo and rode off, but not after again refusing to take any more questions and promising a press release with statements from both he and Dr. Black.

Lamplighter set the VCR to record the channel for another 30 minutes.

"Let's see what their analysts have to say about this," he thought as he grabbed his phone book.

Lamplighter opened it to the Victor/Farmington section to find the name Jeff McLowery. He called the number and talked with Mr. McLowery's wife, Dawn, who agreed to meet him at Saturday's fireworks.

His next targets were Detective Ryne and Sheriff Cornell. Lamplighter knew that they were at the meeting, but he tried to contact them by text anyway. Finally, he made another call to Knight's office and left another message. Lamplighter then watered the plants. The seeds reminded him of time spent working in the garden with his dad. He gave him another call, but it went unanswered again.

It was now 11 a.m., and with his tasks for the morning already complete, Lamplighter decided to take in a nap. He calmed himself down by completing his Wing Chun and cane routines. He set his cell phone alarm for 12:15 and went to bed.

As Lamplighter was closing his phone, Knight was opening up his laptop. On the other end of the videoconference was his friend from New York.

"Sorry for interrupting you," were the first words out of the marketing executive's mouth. "It won't happen again."

"Apology accepted," responded Knight.

"I must commend you on your speech," came the reply from New York. "You kept to the script and showed emotion at the right time."

"I thought it was a nice touch," added Knight.

The two further discussed the press conference. Absalom mentioned that his crew did a good job of picking the woman and making it look like a real kidnapping.

"Of course," added Absalom. "We killed the woman's contact, leaving only the woman, whom we bought off, and the captains who know of the plot."

"Let me guess," added the New York man. "You also lied about the fact that you ran out of chips. I bet you have a whole bunch stored someplace."

"Of course we do," replied Absalom. "When our company delivers them here to Rochester, we are even going to turn that into a media circus."

"And again you didn't talk to the media at the press conference," said the marketing guru. "You should keep that up a little bit longer."

"About that," responded Knight. "I think I want to get into another chess match."

Chapter 23

Lamplighter checked his messages as soon as he got out of bed. As he expected, there was nothing from either Detective Ryne or Knight.

"I have two interviews set up," he thought. "That should make do for the stories, but not for the causes."

Lamplighter had a quick breakfast of cold cereal and a banana. He ate while watching the 12:30 p.m. news. First up was an update on the child that was found Thursday night and the press conference from Knight.

"There goes that liar again," he said to the cat which responded with nothing but a curious look. "I would love to get him for an interview about this."

He ate his meal over the span of 20 minutes as he continued to watch the rest of the news. He especially found it disturbing to learn about both terror groups arrested and riots in some major American cities. The national and world news segment was followed by a car accident in Irondequoit and a fire in Lima. After a commercial, the show returned with a feature on all of the area's fireworks displays. The piece featured an interview with Green.

"This should draw in a crowd," he thought.

The news then segued into a weather report. Lamplighter paid attention to the forecast for both tonight and the weekend. The positive report for both his shift and tomorrow's activities made him smile.

Lamplighter missed the sports report for his morning devotional. He had reached Isaiah Chapters 40-44. The chapters dealt with comfort for God's people. He related Chapter 41, verse 11 with his struggle against Knight and his cabal. "Behold, all they that were incensed against thee shall be ashamed and confounded: they shall be as nothing and they that strive with thee shall perish."

After that, he took a shower. He got dressed by 1:15 and watched some national news as he waited for the ride to his 2 p.m. shift.

Just as planned, Gloria was able to take her break from Dollar General in time to take her husband to work. Lamplighter made sure to be ready in time by preparing his lunch and going through his checklist. All he had to do was a wait.

"Did you remember your recorder?" asked Gloria as she made the final turn into the Wal-Mart parking lot. "You have that big interview."

He double checked by taking it out of his pants pocket and showing it to her.

'Thank you for reminding me," he noted.

Gregg Matzek was just finishing the second hour of his radio show. He was talking about the economic problems caused by the banking problems and related it to a quote by Thomas Jefferson: "I believe that banking institutions are more dangerous to liberty than standing armies. If the American people allow private banks to control the use of currency, first by inflation, then deflation, then the corporations the will grow up around the banks will deprive the people of all property and the children will wake homeless on the continent that their fathers conquered. The issuing power should be taken from the banks and restored to the people to whom it belongs."

"He said that when our country was founded, and look we have today," said Gloria.

"I think about this all of the time," added Lamplighter. "I see signs of it every day."

"Your recorder, milk, Valentine's Day," said Gloria as she parked the car near the employee entrance.

He took a minute to think.

"Three things of which you always have to remind me."

"Correct," replied Gloria right before her husband kissed her.

Gloria headed for home as Lamplighter made a straight line for the time clock. He exchanged greetings with several workers and customers before putting his lunch in the fridge. Lamplighter waited in line for less than a minute before sliding his card through the reader to start his shift. He got a walkie-talkie and inserted his earpiece, then connected the unit to his belt.

Lamplighter generously assisted customers in getting cat food, an outdoor thermometer, small engine oil, hand towels and clay pots before finally making it out to the garden center. Once he got outside, he explained the difference between two grill models and quickly designed a hanging basket.

Department manager Regis and Lamplighter walked around the area to talk about the night's assignments.

"You seem preoccupied," noted Regis as they returned to the register area.

"Good catch," replied Lamplighter. "I have an interview with the sheriff slated for my lunch break. I'm reviewing my questions."

"I can appreciate that," said Regis. "But for now you can keep that busy mind of yours going by working the registers so your coworkers can have their breaks."

Lamplighter spent the next hour waiting on customers. He had a pleasant conversation with Happy Evans. The two used to work together in the sports department of the daily newspaper.

"What can you tell me about the girl found in the pond in Victor?" said Evans, who is a resident of Victor, but works in Canandaigua. "I heard rumors that it is connected to some of the missing children in the area, but our reporters are struggling to find answers."

"Me, too," replied Lamplighter. "I am working on the case from the angle of that girl, plus I was there in Clifton Springs and the sheriff said that it was part of it too."

"Let me know what you find," requested Evans.

"Of course not," laughed Lamplighter. "You are a good friend, but still a competitor."

Lamplighter thought a second has he grabbed the receipt from Evans's order.

"But you still are a citizen of Victor," he said. "And if it helps with the case, I suppose I could let you know. Or maybe not."

Lamplighter invited him to come down to the parade and fireworks. The conversation got the attention of the family next in line, who made a note to get to the lakefront for the festivities.

He spent the next hour working on grills and answering customer questions. Lamplighter recalled lifting two of the medium grills into cars.

"Not a good workout," he thought as he headed back for his 4 p.m. break. "Unfortunately it still was pretty stressful."

Lamplighter took the time to get a sip of coffee and review other papers' stories about last night's kidnaping. He was pleased to see that Knight did not interview for them either. Also curiously

134

missing was any note of connection to the other missing cases from the past couple of weeks.

"One more thing to have to ask the sheriff," he thought.

None of the conversations in the break room interested him, so he scanned the paper for other interesting news.

He helped two customers find merchandise before getting back to the garden center. The second two-hour portion of his shift was a mirror of the previous couple of months, with time spent working on grills, manning the registers and answering questions about plants and landscaping.

Lamplighter gulped down his lunch before heading back outside to interview Sheriff Cornell.

"Just when I said I would get here," said Sheriff Cornell as the two shook hands. "What did you need to know?"

Chapter 24

"OK," started Lamplighter. "How do you know that some of these cases are related?"

Sheriff Cornell tapped his finger on the hood of his car.

"There has to be something that you are not telling me," continued Lamplighter.

"Of course there is," he replied. "That is a good law enforcement trick. If we leave something out of the media, then the criminals will continue to do that thing, whatever that is."

"I get it," said Lamplighter. "That way you can use that in court in order to trap people who you interview."

The sheriff nodded. Lamplighter reached for his wallet.

"Then, we can look for that thing to occur and we can connect them," continued Sheriff Cornell. "If a criminal knows that we are looking for that, then they will stop doing that. It makes our job a lot harder."

Lamplighter took the newspaper's chart out of his wallet, unfolded and laid it out flat on the hood of the car.

"I have marked off the ones that are suspected to have been taken by an acquaintance," he said. "That leaves these."

This time Sheriff Cornell nodded.

"You have already told me that the body you found in Victor is part of a bigger case," said Lamplighter as he put his pen on the listing. "You have also said that the kidnapping that I stopped in Clifton Springs was also related."

Lamplighter pointed out that he had put a star next to them.

"Please put stars on the children that the task force suspects are part of the same ring," asked Lamplighter.

Sheriff Cornell shrugged.

"I guess I could do that," he said, then took the pen from Lamplighter.

He marked every single one that was not crossed off.

"Does that answer your question?" he said as he handed the pen back to Lamplighter.

"Yes," replied Lamplighter. "But now it brings up more."

Lamplighter and Sheriff Cornell decided that they wanted some privacy for their conversation. As a result, they chose to hold it on the east side of the building. The only entrance on that side was for the automotive section. The area also bordered a retention pond, which was protected by a chain-link fence.

In the absence of a chair, Lamplighter took a seat on the grassy area between the fence and the curb.

"Sorry, but the bad leg needs a break," he said. "And not the kind that it had 18 years ago."

Lamplighter took a sip of water.

"Now then, you knew right away that the girl from the Victor pond was part of the same case," he noted. "But how? She was fully clothed and drenched."

"You observed that carefully," noted Sheriff Cornell.

'Thank you," responded Lamplighter. "But here is the other question."

He reached up to hand Sheriff Cornell the list.

"All of those happened in different places. Even the genders and ages are different," continued Lamplighter. "So I ask again. How did you know so fast?"

Sheriff Cornell put his hands on his hips, looked down and tapped his foot.

He was interrupted by a store manager.

"Everything OK here?" asked the manager.

"It's for a newspaper story," responded Lamplighter. "I have a deadline to reach, so this was the only time I could meet."

The manager looked at the sheriff who gave a nod of agreement.

"I will be back on time," said Lamplighter, who checked his wrist watch.

The manager walked away.

"This is why I don't want to tell you," said the sheriff. "You never know where that information is going to go."

Lamplighter put his head in his hands.

"OK, please explain this," questioned Lamplighter. "How did you know that the Clifton Springs incident was part of it since the girls were found alive?"

Sheriff Cornell didn't respond.

"And you also marked the case along Canandaigua Lake," added Lamplighter, who rose his voice slightly in frustration. "Law enforcement never saw the kid."

Sheriff Cornell gave the list back.

"We don't know for sure about that one," admitted the sheriff. "We just know that it wasn't somebody that the mother knew, so we added that to the list."

Lamplighter changed his list to show a question mark on that abduction. He checked his watch again, then put his hand up and wiggled his fingers. Sheriff Cornell helped him up.

"I have to get back," said Lamplighter. "Nobody is around. We have worked together in the past, and you know that I and trustworthy."

Sheriff Cornell paused again.

"All of the kids were branded with a hero sticker," replied Cornell. "We noticed them on the girls from Clifton Springs too."

"Does that tell us that they were put there while the rest of the kids were alive?" asked Lamplighter.

"That's what we think," said Cornell.

"So why didn't the sticker fall off into the pond?" asked Lamplighter.

"I don't know," replied the sheriff. "I am calling divine intervention on that one."

"You are probably right," added Lamplighter. "That's the second time I heard that about this case."

He took a sip of water before continuing his questioning.

"Find out anything else about the victim?" asked Lamplighter.

"I am going to type up a report tonight," responded the sheriff. "I will send you an email."

"Fair enough," said Lamplighter, who extended his hand. "Thank you for your time."

Sheriff Cornell responded in kind.

"My pleasure as always," said Sheriff Cornell. "Remember, what I told you about the stickers was off the record."

"Of course," responded Lamplighter, who headed back to work.

He thought of what his wife had told him about Captain Morgan's purchase from her store. Lamplighter shook his head, then waved the Sheriff back.

"I take it you have more questions," said the sheriff after rolling down his window.

"What do you think of the RFID chips?" asked Lamplighter.

"We have to balance the privacy with the safety," responded Sheriff Cornell. "So right now, I don't know."

Lamplighter turned off his recorder and walked back into Wal-Mart.

Chapter 25

It took Lamplighter only 45 minutes to finish the small grill that was on the department manager's list before tomorrow's expected rush. After that, he took 15 minutes to do a short sweep of the garden center before taking over the greeter role. Lamplighter didn't care for that part of the job too much, except for the fact that it allowed him to meet some interesting people.

"I have a question," asked a lady who Lamplighter guessed was the same age as him. "I just got a dog. Can I bring him into the store to try to find the best size cage for him?"

Lamplighter explained that since the store served fresh food, it did not allow live pets except for service dogs. He offered her the option of bringing the dog into the one of the outdoor plant areas where she could bring the crates out to the dog.

"I guess that will work," she replied. "Thank you."

The woman held the dog by its leash and brought her husband into the store to help find the best crate. Lamplighter called for assistance from a fellow associate in case a ladder was needed to get them off of the top shelf.

The dog turned out to be a poodle. Lamplighter was trying to watch the door while talking with the woman. He observed that the dog looked scared.

"We just got him," repeated the woman, who was now petting the dog. "My husband loves poodles and our last one recently died."

Lamplighter snapped his head around at the woman.

"I know what you are thinking and I caught a lot of flak for that already," she said. "He is not the one that kidnaped that kid Tuesday."

"My wife and I were swimming at the beach at the time," replied Lamplighter. "We were questioned about it, too."

"Like I said, our dog died a couple of weeks ago," retorted the woman, who was showing signs of anger. "We didn't have the poodle at that time."

"You have my condolences," responded Lamplighter in a successful attempt to diffuse the situation.

The woman went on to explain that they had been looking for a new dog and that a friend who was a member of the Rochester Poodle Owner's Club had told her about a classified ad. She agreed to meet with the owner, who then dropped off the dog without a word.

"We got him checked out and the vet said he was going to be OK," she said as her husband came out with the first crate.

"Glad to hear it," replied Lamplighter.

The first crate that the employee brought out was too small.

"How many people are in this club?" he asked.

"We have already been interviewed by the police," replied the woman. "That is what you are trying to do, yes?"

Lamplighter explained his reporter position and how he was investigating the case from the Victor angle.

The husband and employee came back with the perfect-sized crate.

"That's how I remember you," said the husband with a snap of his finger. "That guy from that fight in Clifton Springs."

The employee just smiled.

Lamplighter introduced himself to the husband and told him about the investigation.

"Well good luck on your case," said the husband as they walked toward the registers.

The couple left with a crate. Lamplighter was left with a clue.

"I still think that I should check out the Rochester Poodle Club," the thought.

That thought was interrupted by a familiar voice.

"You missed a great party," said Berry.

"Yeah," replied Lamplighter with a sigh. "Work gets in the way of things sometimes."

"Not in the way for you tomorrow, I hope?" asked Berry.

"I do have a busy schedule, but it shouldn't be a problem," noted Lamplighter as he leaned on a post by the door. "I even think that I will get enough sleep."

Lamplighter continued to explain that his shift was over at 11 p.m. and he still had some writing to do, then added that he had scheduled an interview for his time Lakeshore Park. Berry said that she was there to get some last-minute supplies for the event.

"And I am not going to forget either sunscreen or mosquito repellant," she said.

"I won't get there until 4 p.m. so save some for me," added Lamplighter.

Berry smiled as she went into the main part of the store.

Lamplighter waited at the door for another 30 minutes. There were 16 customers through before Berry came back.

"Got an extra one of each," she said while leaving the building.

Lamplighter manned his post for another 30 minutes before helping clean up the register area and heading back to the break room. He avoided the coffee so the extra dose of caffeine would not keep him awake too long for his early morning parade prep.

The news replayed the feature on the interview with the committee members, but Lamplighter missed any hard news stories.

He spent that last hour of his shift watering plants. He found this the most interesting part of the day, as it left him alone to read labels on the plants and learn about gardening.

Gloria picked him up right on time.

"Sheriff Cornell, a family against RFID chips, and a poodle," said Lamplighter after kissing his wife.

"Ummm I want to say three people you interviewed today," replied Gloria. "But how do you interview a poodle?"

He told the story of the woman and the crate for her new dog as they headed home.

"See, look. There is even a poodle right there in front of the laundry room," said Lamplighter had they parked in their townhome complex's lot.

"That reminds me," sighed an exhausted Gloria. "Can you please help me take up a basket?"

Chapter 26

"Look at him. He's sooo cute," said Gloria as she made a beeline for the poodle.

Gloria got down on one knee and started petting the dog. The dog laid down as she scratched its neck.

"Look honey. He's sooo cute," she said as she looked at her husband.

The poodle responded by wagging its tail. Gloria kept scratching its neck.

"Petting dogs is so relaxing," she continued.

Gloria looked back at Lamplighter and smiled as the dog put its paws on her shoulders. It could get no further toward her since it was tied up to a tree outside the door.

"I think you made a new friend," laughed Lamplighter.

"I told you that animals like me," replied Gloria, who then noticed the animal's tag. "This one's name is Clayton."

He bent over pet the poodle on the back.

"Nice to meet you, Clayton, the dog," he said.

Lamplighter stretched.

"Tell you what," he said. "You can pet the dog. I will get the laundry."

"That sounds great," replied Gloria. "It is the first one in. I left the basket on it."

He walked past his wife toward the townhouse laundry room. It contained four washers and four dryers. Their work schedule demands that the Lamplighters clean their clothes at odd hours at night and into the morning. They rarely see another person in the room.

The room's only other occupant was transferring clothes from the last dryer into his basket. He stopped to fold some clothes on the table. Lamplighter had a clear path to the dryer and went about removing Gloria's laundry.

He could still hear Gloria playing with the poodle.

"Oh you're such a good doggie," said Gloria.

Lamplighter laughed.

"Popular animal," he said to the man, who gave no response but a grunt.

Lamplighter had seen the man before on one of his numerous walks around the neighborhood but never had a conversation with him. He noticed that the man's laundry contained several shirts with football teams - both pro and college.

"Football fan, I see," said Lamplighter.

It finally got a response.

"My favorite sport," said the stranger. "I played in high school and college. I love the sport."

"Me too," replied Lamplighter. "I was a lineman. That is the position I watch the most."

The two continued their conversation until the stranger finished folding his clothes. Lamplighter let him pass, then finished emptying Gloria's dryer. He left the facility only eight feet behind the stranger.

"Awe you have a little lump here," said Gloria as she moved to rub the dog's belly.

"I wish you wouldn't have said that," said the man.

Lamplighter immediately noticed that the stranger reached behind his back. Fearing that he was going for a weapon, he charged as fast as he could. The dog's owner aimed his revolver at Gloria, but Lamplighter was able to hit him in the back just as the stranger pulled the trigger. The gun fired, but the bullet, drifted off into the tire of the Lamplighter's Dodge Neon.

Unfortunately, he couldn't knock the gun from his hand.

"I've read that you were tough," said the man. "But I see you walking around, and pathetically trying to stay in shape."

He then pointed the gun at Lamplighter.

"Let's see how tough you are," he said.

The stranger had to turn his back on Gloria, who took advantage of the opportunity to hit him in the head with her husband's cane.

The man staggered, allowing Lamplighter the chance to grab his attacker's hands in an attempt to wrestle away the gun.

"Tougher than I thought," said the man. "But still not as tough as me."

The man kicked Lamplighter in his bad leg.

"God has blessed me with a high pain threshold," replied Lamplighter, who still refused to let go of his wristlock.

He kept it pointed at the now empty laundry room by twisting the attacker's arm. The stranger fired the gun off again, but the bullet went through the back wall of the facility.

"My next target is your wife," said the attacker.

Lamplighter made him drop the gun by jabbing his thumb into the stranger's wrist. This startled the man. Finding a brief hole in his attacker's defense, Lamplighter kicked him in the stomach.

"That is a better target," he said.

Gloria joined in again with another cane strike to the back of the attacker's head.

"So was that," she said.

The man then fell face first on the sidewalk. Lamplighter sat his 250 pounds on the man's back. Gloria called 9-1-1 but hung up as a city police car arrived.

"You two again," said the same officer that was the first to arrive at Dollar General on Wednesday.

A second officer arrived to help handcuff the attacker. The first cop found a wallet with an ID.

"So how do you know Allan Buchanon?" he asked.

Lamplighter explained that they didn't know him and that everything was OK until Gloria mentioned that the poodle had a lump.

"I'm sure that Detective Ryne will tell you why," said the officer.

A county sheriff arrived and helped put Buchanon into the first officer's car.

"I suppose it is time for another interview," sighed Lamplighter as he put his arm around Gloria.

The Lamplighters spoke with law enforcement for 35 minutes before finally getting into their house.

"Neighbor Matt, that woman from the Salvation Army or somebody else," said Gloria as he took a spot on the love seat next to her husband.

"OK," he said. "I'm stumped."

"Three people who could have called 9-1-1 before me," replied Gloria.

"Good question," said Lamplighter as he patted his wife on the back. "I guess we will find out."

The two relaxed with a sitcom before Gloria started falling asleep in his arms. That was a clue to the Lamplighters that they should so their nightly Bible study. Lamplighter stopped at First Corinthians, chapter 15. The last two chapters of the book dealt with the differences between a spiritual body and a physical body. They discussed chapter 15, verse 52: "in a moment, in the twinkling of an eye, at the last trumpet. For the trumpet will sound, and the dead will be raised imperishable, and we shall be changed."

"You are the trumpet player," said Gloria, referring to his spot in the Salvation Army band.

"It does say that we will be changed," he replied. "But at the last trumpet. That means that everything else is going to happen first."

"So are you saying that we are going to be here for the tribulation?" she asked.

"I look forward to it," said Lamplighter. "We get to see Ken Knight and his group finally lose."

Gloria smiled, then trudged herself up the stairs. Lamplighter followed her but went into the office instead to transcribe the interview with the sheriff.

Lamplighter set the alarm, went to bed, cuddled Gloria, and quickly fell asleep around 2 a.m.

Chapter 27

The Lamplighters had another busy morning. On Saturday, they had to accomplish this on just five hours of sleep.

"Good morning," grunted Lamplighter after they both shook off the shock of the alarm clock.

They agreed to get up at 7 a.m. The plan was to have a good breakfast and clean up a bit before heading out. Lamplighter did his morning devotional and made the meal while Gloria jumped in for a quick shower.

This morning's Bible verses were Isaiah chapters 45-49. The verses described God's confirmation of his covenant with Israel. Lamplighter took heart in the words, reminded of Satan's final defeat. "I have sworn by myself the word is gone out of my mouth in righteousness and shall not return. That unto me every knee shall bow, every tongue shall swear."

He made some scrambled eggs and toast. The two ate while watching a story about themselves on the morning news.

"There we go again," noted Gloria before taking a bite.

"To think," he replied after taking a swig of milk, "if he hadn't pulled the gun on you and just walked away, nobody would have known it was him."

This morning, the news focus was on Buchanon and interviews with members of the task force. The news put up a picture of the Lamplighters while explaining how Buchanon was captured.

"Still," said Lamplighter, "it doesn't explain all the rest of the children on the list, just the kidnapping from Lakeshore Park."

"So there might be someone else out there," noted Gloria.

"Probably more than one," he replied.

He took a bite of eggs and washed them down with some milk.

"That is a frightening thought," said Gloria. "So unless somebody stops them, this is going to go on for a long time."

She drank some milk and a bite of toast that had eggs piled on top of it.

"Not only that, but with so many people they have to have somebody calling all of the shots for them," added Lamplighter, who finished his meal and headed upstairs to get ready for his volunteer tasks.

"With our luck we will run into them, too," remarked Gloria as she brought her dishes into the kitchen.

"So we should always be ready," he replied.

The two left and headed for Gloria's store. The Lamplighters kissed before Gloria entered her store to start another day of store cleaning.

Lamplighter then took the car to Lakeshore Park to get ready for the all-day, city-wide party.

"Glad to see you made it," said Green. "We really need all of that muscle."

The team set up five tents. All of them were the size to cover a picnic table, but had no walls and were ideal for providing shelter while conducting business.

The first to go up was for the sound equipment that would support the day's musical acts. The second was set under a tree at the intersection of the park's two main paths. The goal was to put it in a prominent location for the committee members to check on the festivities.

Both of those tents were held down with rope and stakes. Lamplighter and Gregg Berry, Jill's Husband, took turns stomping the stakes.

"That was fun," said Lamplighter.

"Wait until we get to the next three," replied Berry.

The other three shelters were for food vendors and placed on concrete. This required that they be anchored with a 30-pound weight on each corner.

"I told you this wouldn't be a problem," said Lamplighter as he unloaded the anchors from Green's minivan.

"You should have been here to pick them up from storage," replied Green.

"OK," said Lamplighter. "Mark me down for next year."

The crew took 45 minutes to set up. Lamplighter drove back to Dollar General and parked in Gloria's preferred spot. He walked the four blocks to the parade's staging ground, which was a parking lot across the street from the Sheriff's Department.

"Ah, good. You are here," said Norton while handing Lamplighter a clipboard with the parade entries in the order that he determined.

The then handed Lamplighter a walkie-talkie.

"I've seen you wear one of these at Wal-Mart," said Norton. "I figure you would be good to use it here."

The team was split into three groups. Norton joined the fire police at the main intersection. Area fire departments that made the trip to Canandaigua for the parade assembled in the Dollar General parking lot and were directed by Joe Middleton, another committee member. Norton told either Middleton or Lamplighter how many entries to bring into the intersection. That way, the parade had a good mix of entries from either group.

"Good group of entries this year," said Berry as she joined Lamplighter on the street. "Everyone has their number and is ready to go."

Lamplighter started staging the entries on the street and prepped them on taking the left-hand turn. One-by-one the cacophony of community groups made their way down Main Street. The entries included the traditional scouting groups, local performers and organizations that used the parade as a way to both show off their skills and get new members.

His favorite was a group looking to form a third political party. The group was handing out flyers that echoed a saying they painted onto the side of its float.

"Laws and government are founded on the consent of the people," a brochure noted. It was from a letter from James Sullivan to John Adams.

Lamplighter stood silently for a moment to comprehend the meaning of the statement and relate it to what his investigations are finding today. His thought was interrupted by a familiar voice.

"Wow. I can't believe what happened to you last night," said Mary Caleb, a member of the Salvation Army who lived in the same 55-unit townhouse complex as the Lamplighters. "There were police going into his apartment already at 7 this morning."

"Hey, did you call the police?" asked Lamplighter. "Neither Gloria nor I knew which neighbor to thank."

"It wasn't me," replied Caleb.

That conversation was interrupted by the float's turn down Main Street. Middleton and Lamplighter closed the parade by driving a gator to survey the crowd.

"Good crowd for this," said Middleton when they reached the downtown gazebo.

"I like to see all of our efforts do something for the community," replied Lamplighter.

Lamplighter pretended to talk into his walkie-talkie as Middleton laughed. The two reached Lakeshore Park and dropped off the gator next to the committee's tent. Middleton stayed at the tent to work the first shift. Norton gave Lamplighter a ride home, giving directions to his boat to pass the time.

Matt Waters, who lives in the townhome next to the Lamplighters, arrived in the parking lot at the same time. He headed to his house with the haul from his early morning fishing trip

"Well hello there, neighbor!" exclaimed Waterst. "I still can't believe what happened last night, and right here in our place."

"Me either," replied Lamplighter. "Hey did you call 9-1-1? Gloria and I need to know who to thank."

"Yeah that was me," said Waters. "Right after I heard the gun shots."

"Well, in that case," noted Lamplighter. "Thanks."

Chapter 28

Lamplighter worked on his fighting skills, watered the plants then set his alarm for noon.

He took another shot at calling his dad back in Wisconsin but got a surprise.

"Don?" asked his sister Diana. "What are you doing up this early on a Saturday morning?"

"I'm calling people for stories," replied Lamplighter. "I figured that I would wish my father at happy July 4."

"He's still in the bathroom," said Diana. "He's not doing that well."

Ben is 70 years old and a retired factory worker. He had trouble keeping up the family homestead in Two Rivers, so the family decided to make a switch. Diana, along with her husband, Nathan, and daughter, Emily, moved into the house from a rented property across town. Ben then rented a one-bedroom apartment in a building that was set aside for senior housing.

"He is getting worse, but still sort of healthy," added Diana.

Ben was also a longtime alcoholic. It was because of that fact that Lamplighter decided that he would never drink alcohol. As he drifted to similar friends in college, is served to make his Christian faith stronger.

"I was worried about him," said Lamplighter.

"And we were all worried about you," replied Diana. "We heard about you on the news."

"It reaches that far?" he asked.

Diana explained that a national cable news network had done a story on the child abductions in the area. She added that they even watched a story about Lamplighter taking on the three attackers in Clifton Springs.

"I was there when you broke your leg in training," she said. "How can you still fight?"

"Different style," said Lamplighter. "That was judo. What I do is a combination of strikes" Lamplighter added that he and Gloria were attacked the night before and how it led to the capture of Buchanon.

"So you solved the case?" asked Diana.

"Unfortunately, no," replied Lamplighter. "He was just a henchman. There is something bigger behind this."

"Well, stay safe," said Diana.

"We will, but it's all part of the job," he responded. "Speaking of that, how are things back in Two Rivers?"

Diana gave him the rundown on what was going on with their many cousins, aunts, and uncles, as well as news from the town, including the demolition of a riverside factory that had long been abandoned. In the background, Lamplighter could hear his father coming into the room.

"Well ... Don," said Ben. "Saw you on TV. They talked about you right after they talked about another bombing in the Middle East."

"That just goes to show that the world is a dangerous place," noted Lamplighter.

"Yes it is," said Ben "It sounds like it is far more dangerous for you, too."

"Diana told me all about the story you saw," added Lamplighter.

He went on to explain that he got into another fight the previous night.

"You did all that on that bad leg?" asked Ben.

"I changed my fighting style, some stuff I picked up in Alaska," replied Lamplighter. "That and I stay in decent shape."

His statement prompted Ben to go on a five-minute uninterrupted rant about his own health problems.

"You still stay away from that stuff?" he asked his son about alcohol.

"Gloria and I both do," said Lamplighter.

"Well, good for you," said Ben, who added that Diana was there to pick him up for a grocery shopping trip and a family picnic.

Lamplighter told his father about his adventure directing the July 4 parade and what he and Gloria had planned for later in the evening.

"So that's about it," he said with a loud yawn.

The father and son exchanged pleasantries before hanging up.

"That went as well as it could have gone," he thought as he settled into bed at 10:45 a.m. "God willing, the rest of the day will be just as easy."

Chapter 29

Lamplighter is always short of sleep and appreciated any opportunity to get a rest.

"A nap, a shower and a walk," he texted his wife.

Gloria was on a quick break at her work and was able to give an immediate response.

"My guess is three things that you are going to take," she replied.

"Correct," said Lamplighter. "Now it is time for the nap."

Lamplighter never even remembered falling asleep as the reached over to click off his raging alarm clock. He headed straight to the kitchen for a cup of instant coffee. He prepared a peanut butter and jelly sandwich, then went to work on his two remaining articles.

Lamplighter took the sheriff's quote on RFID chips and used it as the lead for the story, which up until then consisted only of press release statements from Knight and Dr. Black and background information.

"That makes it a little bit better, but not good enough," he thought as he glanced at his recorder. "Today's interview with the family should add the right touch."

His next task was to print out the emailed press releases from Sheriff Cornell and use them in the Victor Pond case. He hoped that there would be enough information from the emails and the interview to put together some semblance of a story.

"Interesting," he thought. "According to the report, the girl was dead before she was put into the water. The estimate is that she had been dead for 12 hours before she was found."

Lamplighter kept typing in the information then organized it into a clear narrative. He then slid in the quotes from Sheriff Cornell. Finally, he noted that the case was connected to others in the area.

This gave him pause.

"How does Allan Buchanon fit into all of this?" he whispered as he let out a deep sigh. "Or does he fit in at all? The poodle only ties him to the Canandaigua kidnapping and not the other three."

He took a sip of coffee.

"Nor was he on the bus Monday morning in Clifton Springs," he grumbled as he tapped his pen on the computer desk.

He went back downstairs to get the phone and call Detective Ryne. Lamplighter started to dial as there was a knock on the door.

"I guess this call is not necessary," said Lamplighter while leading Ryne into a seat in the living room.

He went back upstairs to fetch his recorder for two interviews with the same person.

"I was just working on the case from the Victor News angle," noted Lamplighter. "Just ready to call you, so thanks for stopping by."

Gloria returned from Dollar General for her midday break.

"You are just in time, too," said Detective Ryne.

Gloria took a spot on the couch next to her husband.

"Ladies first," said Lamplighter as he grabbed his wife's hand.

Gloria told her side of the Friday night's fight, then answered the detective's questions. Lamplighter followed by recalling the event from his angle, then took questions from the detective as well. The Lamplighters both then talked about their limited contact with Buchanon. The detective then explained the significance of the lump on the poodle.

"That is one thing that we kept out of the news," he said. "The mother had pet the dog, too, and mentioned the lump."

"That is what I had figured," said Lamplighter. "There had to be some reason why that would set him off."

"He looked different in his sketch," added Gloria. "We figured that he wore a disguise, but that the lump was somehow the only tie to him."

"It looks like you have this figured out on your own," said Detective Ryne.

'Too many cop procedural shows," laughed Lamplighter.

Gloria and Ryne also laughed.

Ryne got up, then thanked them for their time.

"Hold on a second," said Lamplighter as he produced his recorder. "Now it's my turn."

Gloria got up to grab a lunch when Lamplighter clicked on his recorder.

"Now let's tell the readers of the Victor News about the case," said Lamplighter. "They want to know if Buchanon is the person who dumped the child into the pond at the park."

"We are still investigating that," he said. "We are interviewing Buchanon to find out more about the pedophile ring, looking through his apartment for evidence and checking people in this complex to see what they know."

Gloria came back into the room with one cup of coffee each for her husband and Detective Ryne.

She went back to the kitchen table to finish her meal.

Ryne took a sip before continuing.

"We can tie him to the kidnapping here in town," he said before taking another sip. "And we can tie the case to the child in Victor, which ties to the rest of the abductions."

Ryne paused for a second and ran his finger across his notebook.

"But there is no evidence to put Buchanon in Victor," he added. "Unless he confesses to that, but he claims that he wasn't there."

"That doesn't necessarily mean he doesn't know anything about it," replied Lamplighter.

"True," said Detective Ryne. "That is why we are still talking to him."

"So where does that leave that case?" questioned Lamplighter.

"Same stage as before," replied Ryne. "We are still investigating that."

Lamplighter and the detective exchanged pleasantries as they walked on the sidewalk. Ryne stopped to knock on Waters' door.

"Sorry," he said. "I got another interview."

Lamplighter returned to kiss his wife and get back to work on his stories. He immediately transcribed the tape of the brief interview and added some quotes to the story with the sheriff.

"That should do it unless there is another break," he thought.

The last step was the check out the poodle club website.

"Wow," he said as he pushed back in his chair. "I count 11 people that I know."

It was now 2:45 p.m. Lamplighter showered as Gloria took a quick nap.

He dried off while listening to the news. There were neither updates on the case nor more statements from Knight or Black. Instead, they spent a good five minutes talking about overseas drone strikes.

'Well, the Bible does say that the whole world will see the abomination in Jerusalem," thought Lamplighter. "With this and the internet, now they can."

Lamplighter got dressed and Gloria got up at 3:45 p.m. He remembered to bring both a recorder and notebook to get the interview with the McLowery family.

The couple changed plans from a walk to the park. Instead, Gloria dropped him off there. The couple kissed, then Gloria headed back to Dollar General for the evening shift.

"Time for some fun," he said to Green as he took a chair in the committee tent.

Chapter 30

"There is one thing that I don't look forward to doing," said Green. "Canandaigua did not add any extra police for this event."

"So we have to be security, too?" replied Lamplighter.

"That is how it looks," she said. "Oh they are going to come through here on routine patrol and will come if we call them, but basically we have to act as peacemakers. With this big of a crowd, that is something for which we should have added more volunteers."

"The city does not allow alcohol in this park," added Lamplighter. "That is one thing that we have going for ourselves."

"True," replied Green. "But that won't stop some people from bringing it in. Or, getting drunk before they get here."

Lamplighter looked down at his fluorescent green shirt. The team chose that color so committee members would be easily identifiable among the event's crowd.

"We just hope that those who want to cause trouble will respect these," said Lamplighter.

Green laughed while Berry approached to help out at the booth.

"The other option is that they are afraid of you," said Green.

"Well," added Lamplighter. "Either way works."

Lamplighter enjoyed 15 minutes of peace as he tapped his foot to the big band that was performing. The booth did not have any visitors on his shift until the McLowery family showed up for its interview.

"Sorry we are late," said Jeff. "Had to find a parking spot here."

"Not a problem," noted Lamplighter as he stood up to shake the McLowery family patriarch's hand.

Lamplighter took out his recorder and grabbed his notebook and pen off of the table.

"So tell me why you are against these RFID chips," he said.

Jeff McLowery started by handing Lamplighter a pamphlet.

"This outlines our principles and the reasons for our concerns," said McLowery.

Lamplighter gave it a quick glance, then folded it up and put it in a bag under the table, where he planned to keep the rest of his reporter tools..

"How did your family decide to join the group?" asked Lamplighter.

"I always answer that by saying this: 'resistance to tyranny is obedience to God.'"

Lamplighter nodded as he held his recorder up to McLowery.

"Plus," said the father before he was cut off by a crying child.

"Excuse me," said the wife of an elderly couple. "We found this young boy sitting on the grass crying. He said he is lost."

Lamplighter took charge of the situation. He sent Green up to the band in order to make an announcement about the child.

"Make a description and explain where the child can be found, but don't give a name," he instructed her.

He then asked the McLowery family to search on the main path west to the edge of the park and back. Lamplighter gave Dawn McLowery a green shirt and reminded them not to give a name either. He gave Berry the task of manning the booth, the started out on a lap along the river to the boathouse and back.

Lamplighter couldn't find any panicked family on his trip to the building. He heard the announcement when he stopped to search the beach area, then returned to the committee tent on the path through the vendors and the parking lot.

The searches converged on the tent as the child's mother arrived in tears. She held her son, then waited to gain her composure to thank the group. Lamplighter then thanked the couple that brought the child to the tent and rewarded them with green shirts.

"Sorry about that," he said to the McLowerys. "But thank you for your assistance and please continue."

"Glad that we could help," responded the mother. "Funny that happened in the middle of an interview."

"See, some people would use that as an example of how we need RFID chips," continued the father. "The way I see it. It is an example of our community coming together."

McLowery also explained that he was concerned that what he describes as "the wrong people" can use the chips to find the children that they want.

"Why should we make it easier for them?" he asked.

McLowery explained that if the chip can be scanned by the police, then criminals will also figure out a way to scan the tags as well.

"For instance, it works backwards like the ring going on now," continued McLowery "All a skilled computer hacker has to do is program a scanner to find kids that fit the description of the one for whom he is looking and take the kids. It's like having a catalog."

Lamplighter nodded.

"Here is something else to consider," added McLowery. "Those chips will stay in the person for the rest of their lives."

Lamplighter nodded again

"If we get a generation of parents to put them in their children, and the next generation does it as well," said McLowery. "Then the government can pretty much track any citizen at any time without forcing people to take the chip."

The interview lasted through two more songs before Lamplighter thanked the family for the coming down to the park. The two exchanged business cards.

"Don't forget to stay for the fireworks," he said.

"We came here with friends and we already have our spot picked out," responded the mother.

Lamplighter sat down in the booth.

"Now that was multitasking," said Berry.

"All of my jobs are freelance or part time," responded Lamplighter. "I have to do what I can when I can. But thanks."

Upon hearing that, Green left and came back with a surprise - a cheeseburger and soda for all of the volunteers. Lamplighter thanked her and gobbled it up.

At 6 p.m., he sent Gloria a text talking about the missing child. She got right back to him.

"Good thing that you were there," she said.

Gloria added that she was working late getting the Dollar General books ready for the inspection and would probably not make the boat trip.

"But I will try," she said.

"I love you," responded her husband. "You work hard and do your best."

Middleton arrived to add extra help for the night shift. Berry left the booth to help the new band get to the gazebo. The new group was a country music act. The band got through just two songs before Green approached the gazebo again. This time it was for a father who was looking for his missing daughter.

The plan was the same. Middleton continued on to the western edge of the park, Berry stayed in the booth and Lamplighter searched the playground and beach areas. The announcement was heard when he got to vendor area.

"Excuse me," said a teenage girl, who had a leashed poodle with her.

Lamplighter turned around to find a crying girl that fit the description of the missing girl. He walked both the girl and the teenager with the poodle back to the tent. The girl's older sister was left behind at the tent in case her younger sibling was found. They embraced, then used their cell phone to call the father back. The teenager who found the girl apologized for keeping the younger girl when she let her pet the dog.

The father thanked the volunteers. Green responded by saying that they were just glad that they were able to find the child.

Lamplighter walked away from the scene to take a call of his own.

"Is this the Don Lamplighter that keeps bugging me?" said the caller.

Lamplighter checked the caller ID and recognized the number of Ken Knight.

"If you would call me back the first time, I wouldn't need to bug you," replied Lamplighter.

"I will make a deal with you," said Knight. "I will give you an exclusive on the RFID interview if you give me another shot at putting you in checkmate."

Lamplighter paused for a second.

"OK," he replied. "But we have to do it in my territory."

"Name the place," said Knight.

Chapter 31

Lamplighter got a text from Gloria at 8:30 p.m.

"Sorry, sweetie, but I won't make the boat trip. Try to make fireworks."

"OK," he replied. "Meet me at the tent."

"I look forward to it," added Gloria.

"Me too," he said.

Lamplighter made his way to the boat dock on the far end of the park. It was there that he was to meet Norton and take up the rear of the lighted boat parade.

The string of boats was led by the Ontario County Sheriff's Department's rescue craft. The purpose of sending it out first was to cut a path through the flotilla of private boats that were clogging the north end of the lake in anticipation of the fireworks. Directly following the sheriff was a rebuilt two-deck sternwheeler that was used to take tourists on dinner cruises around Canandaigua Lake. Eight more boats signed up to got up behind the larger ship. Each one was decorated like a patriotic float and judged by the passengers on the sternwheeler.

Norton was the only member of the committee who owns a boat. The boat parade was his idea, and he was left in charge of the whole event.

"Welcome aboard," said Norton as Lamplighter stepped into his cruiser. "This is my favorite part of the day."

Norton got back on his walkie-talkie and directed the sheriff craft to take off. Once a safe distance away, he told the sternwheeler to take its place. The procedure was the same for the remaining eight boats.

"It's our turn now," he said to his passengers.

Lamplighter was joined by Paul's wife, one other couple and a third gentlemen. He was introduced to all of them. It was the first time that they had met, but Lamplighter recognized all of them from the poodle club.

He took a look around the craft and knew the brand of the boat as one that was made in Wisconsin.

"I think this boat was made in near my hometown," he noted.

"I thought of that," said Norton. "I thought you might recognize it like I recognize your hat."

Lamplighter had to take off his hat and looked at the logo. He laughed as he noted the trademark of his favorite professional football team.

"That would give it away," he said.

The group started talking about football when it reached the collection of boats waiting for the fireworks. That was when another tradition started.

People started jumping into the water after the boats passed.

Lamplighter took a second look around the boat. That is when he noticed a box full of hero stickers.

"Poodles and heroes?" he thought. "Could he be the ringleader?"

Lamplighter had scheduled a drop-off at the City Pier, after which he would walk the half mile back to the tent to meet Gloria and watch the fireworks. He planned to stay quiet until reaching the dock, then call the sheriff with his theory. To help hide his thoughts from the group, Lamplighter turned around to watch the people jump into the water.

"The sheriff really wishes that they wouldn't do that," said the woman from the poodle club.

"I can understand that," replied Lamplighter. "It's quite a safety hazard."

Lamplighter kept his cane in his hand for the whole trip. He turned around on his knees on the back bench to watch the jumpers.

"But it is kind of convenient for us," said the single male from the poodle club.

Lamplighter tried to understand what that meant, then his head went dark. The unidentified man stood there with a smile on his face and a bloody metal fishing net in his hand

"This is a great plan," said the husband from the club as he and his wife grabbed one leg. "With all of the people jumping in, they will never even notice us dumping one."

Norton's wife and the single man grabbed Lamplighter's other leg. Between the four of them, they were able to get his 250-pound body into the lake.

Norton addressed the group.

"He was involved in three of the contracts for our pedophile league," he stated. "He was getting too close."

The married couple looked back to make sure that Lamplighter was still underwater.

"Let's stick to the story," said Norton. "None of us noticed that he was missing. When we finally did, we remembered that he was talking about jumping in so was just assumed that he did."

Canandaigua Lake is only 12 feet deep this close to the shore on the north end. The shallow water sucked Lamplighter's body straight to the bottom. He had hit the water head first, but since the foursome flipped him into the water by his legs, Lamplighter's body continued its flip and hit the lake's floor foot first. His bad ankle struck a rock at the wrong angle and sent a sharp pain through his body. The pain woke Lamplighter up in time to discover himself at the bottom of the lake with a throbbing headache.

He was always afraid to open his eyes underwater, but the stinging in his foot and the pounding in his head made him forget that. Lamplighter looked around for a spot where light was coming through the water and assumed that there was no boat in that area, but just in case, he held his cane over his head.

"This will hit anything first," he thought.

Lamplighter overcame the agony in his leg and squatted down as far as he could. Just as he had done several times in the 12-foot diving pool at a swim club back in Wisconsin, he pushed himself off the bottom with all of his might. Once he felt safe that he was in the clear, he shot his arms back down to his side for an extra boost.

"Who knew that all of that fun in that pool would come in handy," the thought as his head broke the surface.

Unfortunately, the first thing he noticed was that Norton's boat was still in view.

"Drat, they are still there," he said. "And how did my glasses stay on my face?"

Lamplighter remembered what his wife had said about using the cane as a snorkel.

"Like I said Tuesday," he thought. "I am going to use this the next time."

He shook the cane to make sure that he had all of the water out. Lamplighter then used his hand to cover all but the top hole on the cane, which he covered with his mouth. He dropped himself back under the water with just enough of the handle above the surface that he was able to breathe.

"That should be sufficient," he thought as he stayed under water for a count of two minutes.

Lamplighter instantly started coughing as he once again broke the surface. When that was over, he looked around and began swimming toward the nearest boat.

"Dude, you are bleeding," said a teenager who was the first to see him approaching the craft.

He got his friends to help get Lamplighter on the boat. One of his rescuers got a used sandwich bag and filled it with ice from their cooler. Lamplighter thanked her for it and placed it directly on a bloody bump on his head.

He looked around and asked for help.

"You got a cell phone?"

Chapter 32

Lamplighter was still groggy as he tried to explain the situation to the 9-1-1 dispatcher. A resolution was finally reached as he agreed to meet with city police at the City Pier. Lamplighter wanted to make sure that he would get there, so he handed the phone to the boat's owner and rested with the ice pack on his head.

"Yeah," he said after silently nodding his head for a half minute. "We can take him there."

The parade had already made a path through the fireworks-watching flotilla. Lamplighter avoided being seen by sitting on the floor of the boat. The rescuers made a half-mile journey to the dock complex. Once spotting the city police vehicle, the craft was parked at the nearest tie-up.

By now the parade route had curved away from the area to a path along the west side of the lake.

"Here he is, officer," said the driver.

Lamplighter was helped out of the boat by the officer and two other passengers. He sat on a picnic table to wait for the ambulance. Lamplighter checked his phone and found it was soaking wet and not operable. He got permission to use the passenger's phone again.

"Change of plans," he texted Gloria. "Meet me at City Pier. I'm by the police car."

His next message was to Green.

"I left my recorder and notebook at the tent. Can you keep it for me please?" he requested.

Lamplighter was tempted to call Detective Ryne but thought that the cops would take care of that for him. He deleted Gloria's number from the passenger's phone and returned it.

The police officers took the statements from all of the passengers of the boat, and then let them on their way. Lamplighter, who was fully awake now, told his story to the police.

The ambulance arrived and the emergency medical technician started checking Lamplighter's head. The ice had kept the blood and swelling down, but it still required hospital attention.

"Not again," said Lamplighter. "I already have too big of a bill from that place."

He was interrupted by an enormous hug from Gloria.

"Yes, you are going to the hospital," she said.

"If it happened like you said," reminded the police officer. "We need to take you there for evidence."

"Plus, I suppose I could use that for a lawsuit as well," Lamplighter said.

The EMTs helped Lamplighter get into the ambulance for the two-mile trip to the hospital. Gloria followed in her own car. The Lamplighters sat in the waiting room for the next step. He sent a message to Green to ask her to bring his reporter equipment to the hospital.

Gloria filled out the forms as Lamplighter went into triage. He was brought right into an exam room. The police showed up with a camera and took photos of his head.

Green arrived and dropped off the recorder equipment with Gloria.

"How is he doing?" she asked.

"I think he is going to be fine," replied Gloria. "He is just going to be checked out."

"What exactly happened?" Green inquired.

Gloria looked up at her.

"While I thank you for bringing Don's stuff here, I think you might be too close to the situation to talk about it with you," she responded.

A cop and nurse came out to tell Gloria that it was OK to come into the room. Green stood dumbfounded as to what Gloria meant by her last statement.

"I think you need to talk to her, too," Gloria told the police officer while pointing to Green.

The officer began his questioning.

Gloria went into her husband's room. She also snapped photos of her husband's wound.

The doctor came into the room and started stitching up the cut.

"You got quite a head bump there, but it doesn't look like something serious," he said before running a standard test for concussion.

"I am going to keep you here for another hour for observation," said the doctor. "I think you are going to be fine."

He passed Detective Ryne along the way.

"So what is this big break in the case?" he asked.

Lamplighter looked at Gloria. Detective Ryne nodded that it would be OK for her to be here.

"You remember that you said that all of the kidnapping victims had superhero stickers on their necks?" he asked.

Detective Ryne nodded.

"Well," continued Lamplighter. "One of the last things I remember is a box of those stickers on the boat."

"That might not be enough," noted Ryne.

"There is more," replied Lamplighter. "Every passenger on that boat ... well other than me ... is a member of the poodle club."

"Just like Allan Buchanon," said Detective Ryne.

"Exactly," he responded. "That and they hit me in the head and threw me off the back of the boat. I think they planned that after Gloria and I captured Buchanon."

"Why?" asked Ryne.

"I was getting too close," he replied. "This would have been a great way to get rid of me because of everyone else jumping off the boat."

Detective Ryne got a phone call and left the room. Gloria walked over and held Lamplighter's hand and gave him a kiss.

"Well," said Detective Ryne after coming back into the room. "We arrested the entire group and impounded the boat. We will see what he can see."

With that, the detective left the Lamplighters alone.

"I'm worried about you," said Gloria.

"I was, too until they arrested Norton and his crew," her husband replied. "Now they will have evidence and they don't really need me as a witness."

"I meant about your head," said Gloria.

"Yeah," responded Lamplighter. "Me, too. And I'm worried about the bill."

He was sent home after passing another concussion test. He went right up to his office to get two stories out. He typed in the script of the interview with the McLowery family, and then inserted a couple of quotes into the RFID story. After that, he added some information from the brochure. Finally, he downloaded the photo he took off the family.

It left him two stories to finish. Lamplighter finished the night by emailing his editors with updates on his physical health and the status of the stories.

"OK," he said to Gloria as he took a seat next to her on the couch.

This time the Lamplighters relaxed with ice cream bars and a cheesy alien movie. It, along with the writing, fulfilled the doctor's requirement that Lamplighter stay awake for three more hours.

Their random Bible study started at First John, Chapter 4, where the apostle John compares different types of love. The Lamplighters talked about the meaning of the verses and drew strength on Chapter 5, verse 3: "For this is the love of God, that we keep his commandments. And his commandments are not burdensome."

The Lamplighters finally got to sleep at 4 a.m.

"In, in and in," said Gloria.

"I was thinking the same thing," said Lamplighter. "How long we should sleep."

Chapter 33

"There he goes again," thought Knight while watching the 10 a.m. news. "I really hate that guy."

He was still wearing his Absalom mask to hide his secret identity from the woman who was lying next to him on the hotel bed.

"You up already?" said the prostitute that Madame Stephanie had set him up with for the evening.

"The news never takes a break," replied Absalom. "The more news I know, the more money I can make from my investments."

The woman started to rub Absalom's back.

"Was I a good investment?" she asked.

Absalom waited for a commercial to reply.

"I am quite satisfied," answered Absalom.

The woman kissed Absalom on the shoulder, then looked up at the screen.

"Don Lamplighter," she said, quickly recognizing him from a mug shot on the TV. "Him again. I hate people like that, taking away my business."

Absalom looked at the woman and tilted his head to the side.

"What do you mean by that?" he asked.

"The more people that he converts to Christ, the fewer people that are inclined to use my – um - services," she replied.

Absalom smiled under his mask.

"I'm glad that you have figured that out," he said. "How would you like a job doing other things?"

The woman laid back in bed.

"I'm up for a lot of things," she noted. "What do you have in mind?"

Absalom put the blanket back on the woman.

"Don Lamplighter is the enemy," he said. "But he is not the type that you can kill."

"Why not?" she asked.

"That would do two things," explained Absalom. "It makes him a martyr and starts an investigation. The police talk to his editors; the editors tell them on what he is working."

Absalom stopped his speech to watch the news. The two stayed silent until another section of commercials.

"So?" asked the prostitute.

"Well," continued Absalom. "Then he tells them on what he is working. Police then investigate the stories themselves. That leads them to us."

The woman sat up next to him in bed.

"Then what do we do about it?" she inquired.

"We have to damage his credibility," he responded.

Absalom paused for a while. That pause was extended for another set of news segments. The final news story was about a politician that was involved in a sex scandal.

"That gives me an idea," said Absalom, who walked across the room to grab his cell phone from the table.

"I think I know what you have in mind," she said

The woman laid back on the bed to let Absalom take pictures of her. She stood so they could make a mug shot.

"You stay here," he said as Absalom went into the bathroom to place a call with Madame Stephanie.

"Why are you calling me so early?" she asked. "Aren't you missing the news?"

Absalom took off his mask and laughed. He then took a sip of orange soda.

"I want to run something by you," he said. "A way to get rid or Don Lamplighter."

"I thought you didn't want to kill him," grumbled his prostitution captain.

"The idea is to discredit him," replied Knight. "The woman you selected for me for the evening is very good. I think I have a plan."

Knight explained the idea to Madame Stephanie. The pair hammered out the details for the next 20 minutes.

"But why discredit him now?" asked Madam Stephanie. "Aren't you about to do an interview with him?"

"Good point," asked Absalom. "What do you think?"

"I like the plan," she said. "But about the timing?"

"I'm thinking that Ken Knight looks really good right now," said Knight. "So does Lamplighter."

"True," noted Madame Stephanie. "None of the stories on the RFID chips have said anything about the ideas of the people against the idea. Lamplighter would add that to his piece."

"So you are saying do the interview, then take him down," she asked.

"Yeah," he said. "The interview with him is in public, too."

"Brilliant," she replied.

Knight then called Gabrielle and explained the plan to her.

"Here is what we will do," she said. "I will be right there to coach her. This is spur of the moment, but I think we can pull this off."

Absalom put his mask back on and went out to talk to his woman.

"There is going to be big money in this for you." he said.

The woman smiled.

"We have somebody coming here to help us out," he added.

Absalom changed the channel to a cable news network. It was his favorite show - one that concentrated on money.

"Now get some clothes on for our guest," he said.

Absalom ordered a brunch fit for three people. He hid in the bedroom when the hotel's crew delivered the meal. Gabrielle followed soon after. The three discussed the plans over an impromptu dinner meeting over a small, round hotel table.

"Why are we doing this now?" asked the woman.

"You heard the phrase, the bigger they are, the harder they fall," he said. "Watch the news. Lamplighter is everywhere. If we do this now, it will be a huge fall for him."

"That makes sense," said the woman.

"Besides," continued Absalom. "I have a chess game today."

Chapter 34

The Lamplighters' alarm clock blared at 11 a.m.

"Well," said Gloria as she sat up in bed. "I would say that we slept in as much as we could."

She explained her schedule to her husband. In order to give one of her second assistant managers a day off, she switched the times so she would cover the night shift and her first assistant would take the Sunday morning shift. Gloria was going to work for a while to give the morning shift their breaks.

Lamplighter rolled to his side to check the clock.

"Hey, seven hours," he said. "That is actually a good night's sleep for us."

Gloria laughed then finished getting out of bed to prepare herself for work.

"I suppose I could do some work, too," said Lamplighter, who then followed his wife out of the room.

Gloria took the upstairs bathroom. He walked past her to the spare room office and turned on the computer. He did a quick version of both his Wing Chun and cane practices while his circa 2003 computer booted up. Next, he went downstairs to feed the cat and get breakfast ready for Gloria.

"Wow, English muffins," she exclaimed upon reaching the kitchen

He had prepared a plate with a split muffin, each side topped with peanut butter and grape jelly. He poured her a glass of milk, then dropped another sliced muffin into the toaster. He quickly watered the plants, then came back to finish the meal.

"Are you going to have enough time to finish the stories?" inquired Gloria. "It is getting close to deadline and you still have a shift at Wal-Mart to finish."

"I'll find out in a minute," responded Lamplighter. "I sent emails to both editors last night, or should I say, this morning."

He poured himself a glass of milk.

"I asked each if they would allow me to finish after I got home," he continued. "I still have to more interviews to do today, both of them at Wal-Mart."

Gloria wiped her hands with a napkin.

"Don't forget your recorder," she said.

"Thanks for the reminder," replied Lamplighter. "These last two stories - one on the RFID and one on the pedophile ring - are changing it seems like every hour."

He peeled a banana.

"The interviews are one for each story," he added. "I plan to get done as much as I can, then finish when I come home tonight."

Gloria leaned in as the Lamplighters shared a kiss.

"Well," she said. "Can you sleep in tomorrow?"

"I think so," he responded. "But the way out lives work .... I doubt it."

Lamplighter walked Gloria to the door and gave her another kiss as she left. After that, he finished his breakfast and headed back up to check his emails. Both editors had agreed to extend the deadline. He now had until 8 a.m. Monday to finish his stories.

"At least that is good news," he thought. "I am good at pulling an all-nighter."

His next task was his morning devotional. Today's text was Isaiah chapters 50-54, the topic of which is God redeeming. Lamplighter took comfort in the last verse of the section - chapter 54, verse 17: "no weapon that is fashioned against you shall succeed,

and you shall refute every tongue that rises against you in judgment.

This is the heritage of the servants of the Lord

and their vindication from me, declares the Lord."

Just in case there was an update on the case, Lamplighter listened to the morning news. Again, he was part of the telecast.

"Yep, here they go again," he said.

The newscaster admitted that the details were few, but that catching Norton was a huge break in the case. An interview with the Ontario County district attorney, who sounded very excited that they rounded up evidence, followed.

"Good point," thought Lamplighter. "Catching Norton even means that they can get to go through his apartment for clues. He might not even need information from Allan."

The news showed the same mug shot of Lamplighter that it seemed like they had used every day for the past two weeks.

"Lamplighter is both brave and clever for turning the situation around as well as he did," added Sheriff Cornell.

"And with all that evidence," though Lamplighter. "I am not a target anymore. Or at least for this case."

Lamplighter listened to the rest of the news. It mentioned that a ship was taken hostage somewhere along the coast of Africa.

"Worse and worse," he thought as he headed back up to his office.

Lamplighter got in a good, second read on the pedophile ring story. He added some gaps for quotes from his later interview with Ken Knight. He started to do a proofread on the RFID story but was halted by another knock on the door. It was now 12:30 p.m.

"Hello Mr. Lamplighter," said Officer Bultmant. "I have some more questions for you."

"About last night?" asked Lamplighter, who then let the officer into the living room.

"A different case," said the officer. "There was a woman who reported that she was raped here in the laundry."

"This is the first I've heard of that," noted Lamplighter. "When was that? I've been pretty busy around town and didn't notice anything."

"She said that the guy had a mask on," said the officer, who then put his head down. "But the height and weight are a match for you."

"Then it also matches half of the men in this complex," added Lamplighter.

"That is why I am doing a canvass of the townhouses in here," said the cop.

The conversation was stopped by another knock on the door. Lamplighter looked through the peephole, then let Salvation Army captain into the house. He shook hands with the cop before talking with Lamplighter.

"I heard on the news that you took quite a bump to the head," asked the captain. "When you didn't show up for church this morning, we got worried so I came in to check on you."

"I'm fine," replied Lamplighter. "Gloria and I just wanted to sleep in. That's all."

Captain motioned for his wife, Captain Edith, and Mary Caleb to enter the house. Captain Edith was carrying a casserole dish. Caleb brought in a plate of cookies.

"Thank you very much," said Lamplighter.

"Since we are all here," said Officer Bultmant. "I'll ask all of you if you have seen this woman around here."

He passed the picture of the woman who claimed she was raped. Nobody knew who she was. The officer then read the description of the man for whom they are looking. Not only did it match Lamplighter, but also the captain and the person who came into the room next - Coach Daniel.

"Heard about you on the news," he said. "I was in town and figured I would come over to see about that bump on your head."

"I appreciate you stopping by," replied Lamplighter, who looked around the room. "I count six people in here. I think that is a new record for this room."

Gloria made it seven upon her return from work. That number upped to eight when Matt the neighbor came over to check on Lamplighter right after her. He is also of a similar build to the other three men.

"I can see that I have my work cut out for me," said the officer, who then handed everyone a business card. "If you hear anything, let me know."

With that, he left the room, followed by townhome complex residents Waters and Mary Caleb, who wanted to know more about the case. By now it was 1 p.m. Lamplighter politely asked the rest of his guests to leave so he could shower and get dressed for work.

Gloria leaned in to kiss her husband.

"This sounds like the start of a joke," she whispered. "A Salvation Army captain, discus coach and cop go into an apartment."

Chapter 35

Lamplighter was running late, so Gloria helped out by preparing his lunch.

"Thanks for the help," he said.

"Thank the captain," said Gloria. "All I had to do was put stuff in a smaller casserole dish and put on the cover."

"You had to get the apple and carrots, too," replied her husband. "And put them in the lunch bag."

Gloria laughed.

Lamplighter did his check to make sure he had not only his gear for Wal-Mart, but also for his two interviews. The Lamplighters held hands while walking out to the car.

"You know what I found strange?" he asked after taking a glance at the laundry room. "The police officer said a woman was raped in there, but never said when."

"Probably a trick," noted Gloria. "If he didn't say when it was, and somebody said there weren't there then, then that person is the rapist."

"True," said Lamplighter while nodding his head. "Like they did with the lump on the poodle."

The car radio was left on the same station as Gregg Matzek, but the station was playing gospel music at that time.

"Your recorder, your knife and your earpiece," said Gloria.

"Good start," said Lamplighter. "Three things that I have in my pocket for work."

"Yep," responded Gloria. "Your turn."

"No clue, hmm and when?" he said.

"That's way too vague," replied Gloria.

"Yeah you're right," he said. "But that is what's on my mind right now - when was that woman raped?"

The two played their triples game the rest of the trip to Wal-Mart. The Lamplighters kissed, then parted ways - Lamplighter to the time clock and Gloria back home for a short nap.

He shared greetings with several coworkers and customers on the way to the front registers. He purchased another cheap cell phone and the smallest time allotment available. Lamplighter then headed for the time clock. Once completing his 2 p.m. punch in, he got a walkie-talkie and headed to the garden center. Since Sunday is the least busy day of the week, he only had to help one customer - a teenager looking for a bird feeder - on his way to the garden center.

"There you are," said Green. "We were all wondering about you."

"I'm doing fine," replied Lamplighter, who then pulled his recorder. "Thank you again for bringing me this. I have two interviews here."

"For the pedophile story?" asked Green. "I feel so embarrassed that he was part of our committee."

"Me, too," added Lamplighter. "But we had nothing to do with the ring. If he weren't part of the group, he wouldn't have invited me on the boat and we never would have been able to break this open."

"Good way of putting it," she replied.

Lamplighter helped Green find the color and type of mulch that she needed. She was one of only eight customers that came to the garden center over his first two hours.

Lamplighter used his first break to review any stories about the ring. Both of the papers had stories. One of the articles noted that the boat was impounded. He made a mental note to ask the sheriff about that. The television recalled that Lamplighter was shoved of off the boat.

"That happened to you?" asked an associate from the shoe department. "Too bad this is far from over."

"I thought they said that they think he is the leader of the ring," asked an associate from the deli.

"He might be," replied Lamplighter as he took the list out of its wallet. "But now we have to find who else was involved and who did what to what child. The results will be disturbing."

With that, Lamplighter headed back out to the garden center. He encountered not a single customer along his way.

The next two hours were even duller than the first section. Lamplighter spent the time between cashing out four customers and cleaning up the grill and furniture sections. While doing so, he passed the time by thinking of what chess moves he could use in his upcoming contest.

Rain started falling heavily when the black limo pulled up into the parking lot. Lamplighter and the other two members of the garden crew pulled down the canopies and enjoyed the sound of the water droplets hitting the patio's metal roof.

"So now what are we going to do?" asked one of Knight's bodyguards.

Lamplighter looked around the garden center.

"We will set up there," he said as he pointed to a section that was used for the display of patio furniture.

Lamplighter then looked at the clock on the register.

"6 p.m.," he said. "I will be right back."

He returned to the garden center with a cup of coffee, an apple, the casserole and the chess board.

"Game first, then interview," Lamplighter said, then set up the board.

They had previously sent text messages to agree on the ground rules. It would be a game with 15 minutes per player. They would decide who would get what color with a coin flip.

"Strange place for an epic battle like this," said Knight.

"I thought this would be a great place to grill you after the game," responded Lamplighter with a grin.

Knight and his bodyguards groaned.

"OK, we agreed," said Knight. "No talking during the game."

Knight chose white and opened with the E5 system. Lamplighter just nodded, then countered by making an equal move with his pawn. Knight built a three-minute time advantage by scripting his first 10 moves while Lamplighter, who based his strategy on no strategy, needed more time to think through each play.

The two exchanged one rook, one bishop, and two pawns. After 17 moves, the board looked similar to their contest on Monday. Recognizing this, Lamplighter made a different move. This caused Knight to stand up in frustration.

Lamplighter opened his casserole dish. One of Knights guards glared at him.

"This is my lunch hour," replied Lamplighter.

Knight quickly turned his head to Lamplighter, who then put another spoonful of the meal into his mouth.

Knight then looked at his bodyguard.

"Impolite but not against the rules," he said. "At least he is eating with his mouth closed."

He took a deep sigh and shook his head in disgust. He took another two minutes to make a move.

Lamplighter took the opportunity to gradually close the time gap.

After move and counter move, the game was left tied as both players had four minutes remaining and had the king, queen, rook, bishop and pawn on their side. Lamplighter finally made a mistake, leaving Knight with one rook with two minutes to play.

Lamplighter put the half-finished casserole on the floor next to him.

"Now I have to concentrate," he thought.

That is when Knight picked up the pace. By making moves twice as fast as Lamplighter, he was able to build a 35-second advantage. But the faster pace frustrated Knight, who left himself open to a discovered check. Lamplighter reached to make the move, only to run out of time.

"It appears that I win again," said Knight. "But I must admit that you gave me a great battle, but just like last time, you ran out of time."

"Thank you for the game," replied Lamplighter while reaching into his pocket. "Now for the interview."

Lamplighter had one goal for the interview. He wanted Knight on the record saying what he thought about people who are fighting against the RFID system. Lamplighter politely listened as Knight responded to intentionally easy questions.

Lamplighter had wanted to start out with the softball questions, then he finally asked what he wanted to know.

"Do you get any financial gain from this?" he asked.

"Well, no," replied Knight. "I am giving these away for free."

"Fair enough," said Lamplighter. "But what do you say to those that claim that the chips are part of a trick to get people to accept a control grid, like the mark of the beast from Revelation?"

Knight laughed.

"You know, there is absolutely no truth to those rumors about me having an agenda for these chips. Do you know that right now this store is using them to track their inventory?" he said as he stood up. "Look, conspiracy theory people are just a bunch of crackpots. The earth is round, cigarettes cause cancer and I have no hidden agenda with the RFID chips."

Knight then left the garden center.

"Goodbye, Mr. Lamplighter," he said. "I hope we get a chance to play again."

"Somehow I think we will," replied Lamplighter, who then took another bite of his meal and chased it with a sip if coffee.

He watched through the door as Knight's bodyguards led him back to his limo. The rain let up just as the door was shut after him.

Chapter 36

"That's him, that's him," yelled a young woman running across the Wal-Mart parking lot. "That's him. I swear it's him."

The woman was on a beeline run from the garden center to Sheriff Cornell.

"How may I help you?" said Cornell after tipping his cap.

"I just went through the garden center checkouts," said the woman after taking deep breaths.

"Take a rest," said the sheriff. "Then explain to me what happened."

"I just saw the guy who raped me," she said. "That guy. I will know him anywhere."

Sheriff Cornell put the woman in the back of his car. He explained the plan. Sheriff Cornell drove past the door of the garden center to allow the woman to get a good look from his car. They would then head to a different place in the lot and talk more.

"They are expecting me," said Sheriff Cornel, who had an 8 p.m. appointment to walk around the store with Lamplighter. "So this will be no big deal to see me."

Cornell executed his plan.

"It's him. It's him," she said from the back seat as they traveled past the sliding glass doors. "That guy."

Vic and Gabrielle watched from a strategically parked car.

"This better work for her sake," said Vic.

"Relax," replied Gabrielle. "If this doesn't work, we will just dump her in Absalom's incinerator and problem solved."

"Except for the Lamplighter problem," noted Vic. "Boss wants to ruin his credibility instead of killing him."

He cracked his knuckles.

"Darn," he added.

"Then how do you think we can take care of him?" asked Gabrielle.

"Not sure," said Vic. "Boss is scared that Lamplighter is going to make him look bad in the story."

"That is why we are here to do the interview with him," said Gabrielle. "To try to make the boss look good."

"I heard that he made a good impression," said Vic, who noted that he sent one of his agents through the garden center in disguise as a customer. "If Lamplighter makes him look bad, the boss will have to try something else."

They watched as Sheriff Cornell kept going past the doors and headed to the back part of the lot. Cornell asked the woman for a quick review of the rape.

"Which guy did you say did it?" he asked. "The worker with the glasses. His name tag said 'Don.'"

"And you said that you were raped in the laundry room Saturday morning?" asked the Sheriff.

The sheriff called up her case on the computer. He then got out of the car and called the Canandaigua City Police for clarifications. The officer who was working on the investigation confirmed the woman's story.

"Here's the thing," said the sheriff. "She pointed out Don Lamplighter. Wasn't he at the parade at that time?"

"Oh yeah," replied the officer. "As the staging director."

"So it wasn't him?" inquired Sheriff Cornell.

"No that is a pretty rock-solid alibi," replied the officer.

Cornell explained the situation to the woman. He dropped her off at her car and told her to call him at the Canandaigua Police should she have more to add.

"They didn't arrest him," said Vic. "In fact, they didn't even talk to him before letting her go."

"OK, something went wrong," said Gabrielle.

Absalom's captains decided to follow her. When she finally got to her house in Rochester, Vic and Gabrielle invited her into their Cadillac.

"We need to get to Absalom's for a debriefing on this situation," said Gabrielle, who was sitting in the back seat.

The woman complied.

"You gave me bad information," she said.

"How so?" asked Vic, who was driving.

The woman grabbed a sip from her water bottle.

"I worked out the plan. I waited for Lamplighter to get on the register, then checked out through the garden center," she said.

"That is what we told you to do," said Gabrielle.

"But you told me to say that I was there Saturday morning," said the woman. "I did that, but Lamplighter wasn't sleeping in like you said he would be."

"Our informants say that he sleeps in and would be alone because his wife worked at that time," noted Vic.

"But he wasn't," replied the woman, who added that she overheard the sheriff. "Apparently he volunteered to work at a parade that morning. He doesn't even have to prove that since the staging area was across the street from the Sheriff's Department. They saw him there."

"I apologize for that," said Vic. "I have to talk to my sources."

"So what is going to happen to me?" asked the woman.

The group reached Knight's mansion, after punching in the gate code and getting a wave from a guard, they went right up to the main door of the house.

"Our boss wants to use more of your services," said Gabrielle.

"That's sounds like fun," said the woman.

The trio was met at the door by Knight and Madame Stephanie. They led the woman into the basement, where Absalom put on his mask and shot the woman twice in the head.

"So sad," said Madame Stephanie. "She was one of my most profitable girls."

Absalom shrugged.

"We were going to have to kill her anyway," replied the leader. "That is the key to keeping a good conspiracy."

Her body was placed in the incinerator.

"Now that was a good investment," said Absalom. "Gets rid of my problems and provided good fertilizer for my garden."

"Why don't you just get what you need from Don Lamplighter at the garden center?" laughed Vic.

"That would be a great way to keep an eye on him," noted Absalom." It looks like we have to step up our surveillance again."

Chapter 37

Lamplighter stared impatiently at the clock on his cash register. He had an 8 p.m. visit scheduled from Sheriff Cornell. It was now 8:45 and he hadn't heard from him.

"This is a double whammy," he thought. "It probably means that he is out doing his job. I hate to be selfish, but I do need that interview for my last story."

Lamplighter bided his time by watering the indoor plants. He got through the green accent potted plants on the shelf and started to refill his pitchers when Cornell finally walked in.

"Sorry about that," said Sheriff Cornell while walking toward Lamplighter.

"I've got a funny story for you," he said just as he got near the water spigot. "Somebody just accused you of rape."

"I fail to see how that is funny," retorted Lamplighter.

"That part is neither humorous nor ironic," said Sheriff Cornell. "This is the part that is. She said it was Saturday morning. You don't even need to give an alibi because some deputies saw you in the parking lot staging the parade at that time."

"OK," said Lamplighter, who then nodded his head. "That part is both ironic and humorous."

"I went and checked with Canandaigua Police," continued the sheriff. "They did a canvass of the townhouse and nobody saw anything."

"I was part of that," responded Lamplighter. "There were four people in my apartment at that time that fit that description."

"It gets more interesting," said the sheriff. "They got a look at the security cameras for the area. Not only do they not show rape, but they do not even show that that woman was there."

"What about the laundry room?" asked Lamplighter.

"They did a sweep of that, too," replied Sheriff Cornell. "Found no evidence of a sexual event, let alone rape."

Lamplighter finished filling the pitchers and set them all up on a cart.

"So does that tell us that she made up that story?" he said.

"That is what we think unless she shows up again," said the sheriff.

It was now 9 p.m. and time for Lamplighter to start locking up. The two talked as he performed the tasks on the nightly checklist. The manager came down to lock the doors to the outside, looked at Lamplighter talking to the sheriff and just shook his head.

"But why would somebody do that?" said Lamplighter, who paused while tapping his pen on one of the registers. "Was I the only one accused?"

"That is what I understand," noted Sheriff Cornell.

"So," asked Lamplighter. "Can we assume that I am a target again?"

"I suggest that you be careful," replied the sheriff. "Somebody might want to stop you from doing your stories."

Lamplighter pulled out his recorder.

"Let's go talk while I head to the break room," he said.

"Of course," said the sheriff.

The sheriff explained the situation. Since it was such a big case, a team of experts was called to swab the boat and found blood. Once Norton was told that he asked for his lawyer. He added that Allan Buchanon told the sheriffs that Norton was the ringleader of everything.

"Did anyone admit to the dropping off the girl in Victor?" asked Lamplighter.

"Here's a scoop for you," said the Sheriff.

He went on to explain that Buchanon had outlined how the procedure worked. He would get the kids and bring them to Norton. He even made the connection to the poodle club, just like you did.

"But we don't know what happened from there?" asked Lamplighter.

The two had reached the employees only door. Lamplighter invited the sheriff to come in and chat near and employee bulletin board, explaining that it would be better than talking in front of customers.

"Yes we do," said the sheriff. "Remember the people on the bus in Clifton Springs?"

Lamplighter nodded.

"Well," continued the sheriff. "They explained it from the other side, including how they got a hold of Norton to take an order and even a rumor they heard at one of their clubs. They heard that the child in Victor was shipped to a businessman in Honeoye Falls, who dropped her in Victor to throw us off."

"How did that go?" asked Lamplighter.

"Glad you asked," said the sheriff. "We got him at his house. He confessed and named Norton as well."

"So it looks like we got everyone in the ring," said Lamplighter. "That's good news for the area."

"And it is news for you for the Victor case," added the sheriff.

"Yeah," sighed Lamplighter. "That, too."

They then discussed the fact that there was no evidence that tied the ring to Knight.

"Got anything else?" asked Lamplighter.

"The only thing I want to say is that I thank the residents of the area, as well as all of the police and other government agencies that helped with the case," he said.

He told Lamplighter that he had emailed more press releases. Lamplighter thanked the sheriff, then went and filled his coffee mug and watched the TV news reports.

"Ha," he thought. "I know more than them."

Lamplighter finished his shift and let out an enormous sigh of relief as he got into the family car.

"You look tired," said Gloria.

"Yeah," replied Lamplighter. "So do you. That is what we get for working hard."

"But we still have work to do," noted Gloria.

"True," he said.

The Lamplighters shared a light snack and a funny animal show before their random Bible study. Gloria landed Mark chapter 13, which is considered one of the most prophetic chapters of the Bible. Lamplighter made a note of verses 5 and 6: "And Jesus answering them began to say take heed that no one deceives you. For many will come in my name saying 'I am he' and will deceive many."

"That sounds like what Knight and his ilk are doing," remarked Lamplighter.

"I was thinking that, too," replied Gloria.

Gloria headed to bed, and Lamplighter went to the office.

He first transcribed his interview with Knight and added three quotes to the RFID story. He then applied his four-part editing procedure and sent the article to the health magazine.

"Darn it," he thought as he sent off the story. "This is a horrible ending to the week. Yes, the pedophile ring was stopped, but other than theory, I still have nothing to get Knight."

The computer flashed that the message was sent.

"There is another $100 for our bills," he whispered. "I had to be fair, but it would be better if I could find something out about Knight."

Next, he printed out the press releases from the sheriff and transcribed the quotes. Lamplighter rewrote the story to lead that Norton was caught and faced several charges in the ring and that the suspected who dropped the girl into the Victor Park pond was still at large. After pushing the story through the four steps, he sent it off to the Victor News editor.

"At least that case is finished," he said.

He crawled into bed and put his arm around his wife.

"Glad this week's over," he thought.

Chapter 38

Absalom donned his mask for yet another meeting early Monday morning.

"I've been watching you," said the female voice in her British accent on the other side of the video conference.

The woman sat with her two children and her group of seven selected elders.

"I must admit I am impressed," she added. "I never knew you were such a good public speaker."

Absalom sat alone in his inner sanctum that consisted of a bathroom sized main room off of the conference center in his east-side Rochester mansion.

"I've had good coaching from my grifter and my prostitution captain," he responded.

"You choose your minions well," said the leader. "I have a lot of hope for you in our organization."

Absalom's sanctum featured five computers, each displaying a different website ranging from financial areas to comic book sites. He had four televisions - one for each of the three major cable television news networks and one for the 24-hour news channel.

"You spend way too much time watching the news," she said. "You will end up with depression.

"I see it like chess," replied Absalom. "That is how I get ideas for what to do with all of our investments."

He leaned back in his chair and assumed his favorite power pose.

"Plus," he added. "I like to watch the parts of our plan come together."

"That is why I summoned you here tonight," she noted. "To tell you more of the plan."

"I'm interested," he said. "But why tell me so soon? I'm just on the bottom of the food chain in your group, Number 119 out of 120 if I recall correctly."

"True," replied the leader, who then turned around to look at the group's symbol, which hung behind her. "You know the overall plan."

The same symbol was above Absalom's head. He positioned the camera so it will be visible during the conference.

"Yes it's a two-step process," he responded. "Create the crisis, then come in as the peaceful leader."

"Correct," said the woman.

"Just like I am doing with the RFID chips," he said. "Except we were lucky and didn't have to create the crisis."

"You are doing a great job with that," said the leader. "You have positioned yourself well as a philanthropist. Nice touch."

The seven council members and the children nodded in response.

"But the one difference is this," she said. "Well, like you said. You took advantage of a crisis with the missing children, good move."

"Thank you," replied Absalom.

There was a pause as one of the committee members whispered into the leader's ear.

"I have just been reminded. How did it go with Don Lamplighter?" she asked.

Absalom explained how the plan had failed, but that they got rid of the girl.

"I think I played myself in a good light though," he added. "I tried to end the career. But instead of ruining Lamplighter, I used him."

"You did a good job of learning from us then," said the leader.

"Thank you." replied Absalom.

"But this time you are going to help us create the crisis," she said.

"Given my talents, I think I know what you have in mind," he replied.

"There is something else," added the leader. "Did you notice that there are now eight candidates for U.S. president? Well, you are going to help us rig it."

The leader explained the details of the group's plan. Absalom nodded to every word.

"I can do that," he said.

"Good," replied the leader. "I was glad to hear you say that."

The two exchanged chitchat for another 15 minutes, mostly to make fun of the people of the world, who are completely unaware of the plot.

"One more thing," added Absalom. "I beat Don Lamplighter in chess twice this week."

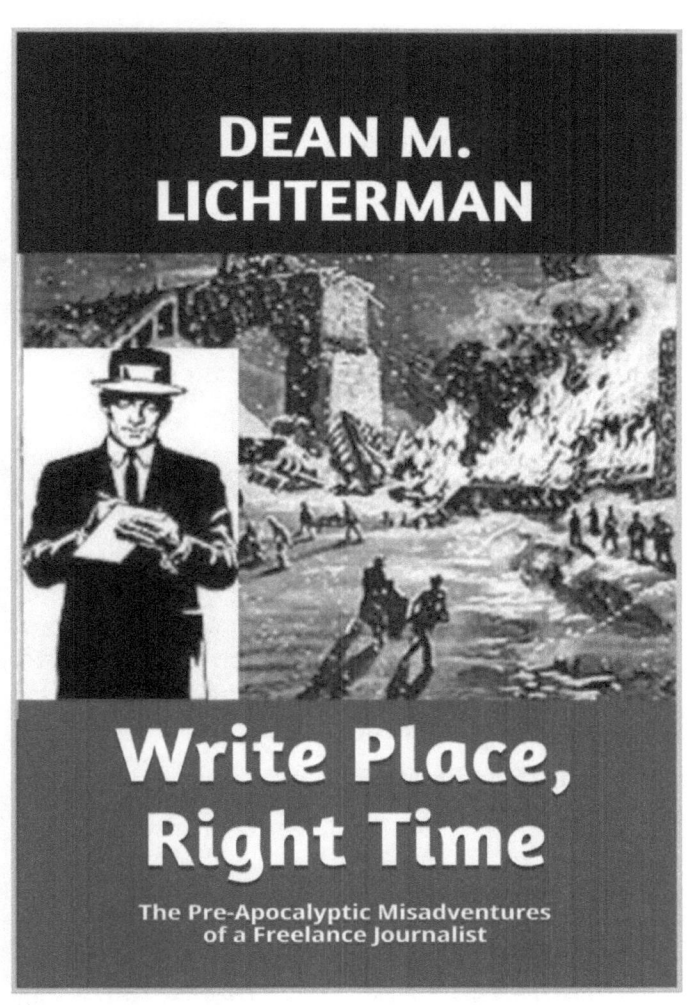

DEAN M. LICHTERMAN

Write Place, Right Time

The Pre-Apocalyptic Misadventures of a Freelance Journalist

Attributions

Thank you for reading "Cane and Able." The quotes in the book come from a variety of sources. Here is where I found them:

Chapter 3 - "Man is born free, but everywhere he is enslaved," said Matzek in reciting Rousseau.

The American Heritage History of The American Revolution by Bruce Lancaster

Chapter 5 - "Let me start with a quote from Plato," he said. "This and no other is the root from which a tyrant springs; when he first appears as a protector."

The website Brainy Quotes

Chapter 7 - "This one is from the mayor of Chicago - You never let a serious crisis go to waste. And what I mean by that is an opportunity to do things you think you could not do before."

The website Brainy Quotes

Chapter 9 - "We fight, get beat, rise and fight again."

The American Heritage History of The American Revolution by Bruce Lancaster

Chapter 15 - " How about Thomas Paine; Our citizenship in the United States is out national character. Our citizenship in any particular state is only our local distinction. By the latter we are known at home, by the former to the world. Our great title is Americans."

The American Heritage History of The American Revolution by Bruce Lancaster

Chapters 17 - "Tis God that girds our armor on and all our just designs fulfills; through Him our feet can swiftly run and numbly climb the steepest hills."

The American Heritage History of The American Revolution by Bruce Lancaster

Chapter 17 - "The Revolution was effected before the war commenced. The Revolution was in the minds and hearts of the people ... This radical change in the principles, opinions, sentiments and affections of the people was the real American Revolution."

The American Heritage History of The American Revolution by Bruce Lancaster

Chapter 19 - Lamplighter remembered a story he had done regarding new guidelines for CPR. According to the rules, if you know when the person fell, you only have to perform what is called hands-only CPR, which is 100 chest compressions per minutes without rescue breathing.

American Heart Association website.

Chapter 23 - "I believe that banking institutions are more dangerous to liberty than standing armies. If the American people allow private banks to control the use of currency, first by inflation, then deflation, then the corporations the will grow up around the banks will deprive the people of all property and the children will wake homeless on the continent that their fathers conquered. The issuing power should be taken from the banks and restored to the people to whom it belongs.

Chapter 28 - "Laws and government are are founded on the consent of the people," a brochure noted that it was from a letter from James Sullivan to John Adams.

Revolutionary summer, The Birth of American Independence by Joseph Ellis.

The statistics on child abduction are from an article on the New York Times website date March 8, 2013.

In the book, I use the English Standard Version (ESV)

The Holy Bible, English Standard Version Copyright © 2001 by Crossway Bibles, a publishing ministry of Good News Publishers.